I0746009

MODERN
FOLKLORE

Modern Folklore
Daniel Perry

This is a work of fiction. Any similarity to actual persons, living, dead, undead, or actual events is purely coincidental.

 @littleghostsboo

 @littleghostsbooks

Published by Little Ghosts Books.

Visit us at littleghostsbooks.com

Cover Designed and illustrated by Chris Krawczyk.

Edited by Chris Krawczyk & phillip rowan

ISBN: 978-1-7389097-5-9

à Pauline, depuis 10 ans

je pus enfin me distinguer complètement, ainsi que je
le fais chaque jour en me regardant

*They come down in the night
These women
sucking the very life out of me As lustful
themselves as my schemes are
and as cruel*

—John Newlove, "Succubi"

I PARKED MY TRUCK near Hugh's new apartment and took the Bathurst bus and streetcar to Dundas, where, a few steps west, a bar had migrated upstairs from a street-level pub into a hollowed-out office space. A crude stage had been built at one end of the cavity, an unsteady plywood bar at the other, and between them were clustered a good two-hundred dirtbags—long-haired, pierced, tattooed, black-clad—the frontmost of them seething in strobes and roar.

It was around ten-thirty; late, but still early at a metal show. With a large beer in each hand, I edged my way to Jeet, who stood half a foot taller than everyone and was easy to spot. His girlfriend, Hisayo, mostly ignored me, but Jeet slapped my palm and said the band was only the second. Two more would follow. On stage, the shirtless singer had covered his face in blood I could tell was fake, but the goat skull he drank from looked pretty real. I crushed the beers to catch up and had just thrown the cans onto the floor when from behind a shoulder smashed me into the pit; I looked back before the wildmen started me pinballing and saw our metalhead buddy, Anthony, staring me down. I managed to free myself when the screaming instruments all cut at once and, sweaty now, I returned to the bar. I thought I'd find Hugh on the way, but after I paid and worked my way forward again, I still hadn't seen him.

I asked Jeet, who motioned to the back of the room. "He went over there with this girl we know."

"Oh yeah?"

"We don't *know* her," Hisayo said, scowling. "We've just seen her at a couple of shows."

"I'm supposed to stay at his place tonight."

"You can't stay at ours," she said. She kept her eyes on Jeet, who didn't argue.

"I'll figure it out," I said. "It's fine." I took out my phone and texted him.

Dude, where are you?

Beer three was empty and I moved on to the fourth. I scanned the room behind us again, but didn't see him. The next band started playing and I thought for sure Hugh and the mystery gal would join us, but when they didn't, I looked back once more and finally spotted him. I'm pretty sure it was him. He was pale and seemed unsteady and was being led to the exit by a woman or, at

the very least, someone with long, dark hair. I handed
my beer to Jeet and tried to get to them, but by the
time I'd pushed through the crowd, descended the stairs
and gone out the door, all I saw was a cab pulling away.

Good for him.

Back inside I reclaimed my can and finished it. I
might have stopped drinking then, but Hugh was going
to need some time. I grabbed another round—another
two-fer—and watched the rest of the show. As the final
band wound down, I reached for my phone again. He
hadn't replied. I wrote, *Leaving soon.*

A bit later, I added, *On my way to your place*

Cab's at Bloor

Pulling up

Still no reply.

His name wasn't on the buzzer panel, probably
because he'd just moved in, so I rang number ten and
woke someone else, who wasn't impressed; I'd
forgotten that unit and buzzer number never match, it's a
security thing. I called his cell, but after three rings it went
to voicemail. I sat down on the steps to think.

Hugh had essentially disappeared when he and
Christine got together, and now it was happening again.
If he didn't come home, I'd have to sleep in the truck. I
stood up, walked to where I had parked, and got into
the passenger seat; if a cop came and I was on the
driver's side, I'd have "care and control" even if I wasn't

awake. They'd give me the breathalyzer, too, which I wouldn't have passed right then. I tossed the keys under the running board for good measure—best to not have them on me at all—then pulled the door shut and balled up my jacket against the window, where I rested my head and let my feet dangle over the console.

Later, my phone woke me and I thought, *Hugh. Finally.* The screen, however, read *Kate.*

When I answered, she said, "The baby's coming."

Here it was: the straw to break the camel's back. I said the only thing that made sense to say.

"I'm sorry."

"*Excuse me?!*"

"I can't drive yet. Can you call Trish?" Kate's sister had been on standby in case the baby came while I was at work or something. She'd pick up Kate, and drop our son Cole at their parents', and get Kate to the hospital in plenty of time, but I'd still have to hear it.

Bobby got drunk is not *what we made the contingency plan for.*

I wanted to remind her that Cole took thirty hours—as though she could forget—and that nothing was likely to happen before morning, but I'd also heard from a few friends that the second comes faster. I stayed mute, thinking of what to say. Kate filled the silence.

"You're an asshole. Couldn't you go one night without drinking?"

My voice cracked as I said again, "I'm sorry, Kate."

She said nothing.

"I'll sleep a couple of hours and call you when I'm on my way. Hang in there."

She scoffed. "Hang in there. Yeah, thanks."

"I love you," I said, and I felt tears in my eyes.

Kate hung up.

I could go a night without drinking, just not then. Now I've gone four years and learned my triggers.

I wound up in the program because what happened next is, I lay there not even ten minutes before I said, "Fuck it," and jumped out to get the keys. I was starting to sober up, or at least I thought I was, and I'd driven the highway home a thousand times. I wasn't going to let a couple of beers be the reason I missed Emily's birth—or more importantly, wasn't there for Kate, for which I already knew she'd never forgive me, as was confirmed after I turned onto Bathurst, found a R.I.D.E. checkpoint down the hill at Davenport, walked the line then blew a zero-point-zero-six, in the warn range.

I didn't go to the hospital that night. I went to the police station.

SATURDAY

UNTIL A FEW PAGES FROM NOW, when I drive away after helping Hugh move into his apartment, I'm part of the story—a side character, but I'm there. After that, relevant messages are reproduced verbatim, and conversations in-person or on the phone recalled to the best of my ability, but where you don't see me with him, I'm inferring at best and, at worst, outright making it up. You can understand, though: I've heard nothing from Hugh—not an email, a text, nothing—since the part a little before the end where he doesn't pick up my call. I don't know where he lives now. I suppose I don't know *if* he lives. I don't use social media anymore and he must not either. I've searched his name on the internet from time to time in the last few years, but turned up nothing. And I can't just dial his number. Kate and I agreed: if she took me back, I could never contact him again.

Hugh and I were close when we were skinny kids in high school, both of us pretty indistinct except maybe for Hugh's acne. After he left for college, though, just an hour's drive from where we grew up, I didn't see much of him—and not at all after he finished, not until he called me out of the blue on a late-September day, needing help to move out of the house he'd shared with Christine. They'd been together nine years, but I'd still only seen her in photos; she curled her blonde hair for occasions, but tied back a lump of frizz the rest of the time. I knew nothing about how they got together, just what Hugh said on the phone about how it had ended, but he needed a hand now and I didn't hesitate. All I had to do was drive into the city from Burlington, which I'd been doing for years already, working in film, leaving crazy-early in the morning for a few weeks at a time and then sitting on my hands the next few, waiting for the phone to ring and the cycle to start again.

I was let into the union a few years ago as a craftservice, which a lot of people think means I serve food, but the name's a catch-all. I got started by following Jeet, who I've known since my first month at university. I'd loved horror movies since I was a kid, so I joined a club, and when I met him he was already making his own shorts—slashers and Satanists and psychological stuff, too, one after another. I helped him with a student festival entry and did kind of whatever he asked, dicking around with fake blood or firecrackers and ignoring that I had no idea what I was doing, getting by on just instinct, teenage shitty job experience, and what I found on the internet about DIY special effects.

It was fun, but it was done by November, and then there were exams and Christmas and snowstorms until slack week, when I took the bus home on a Friday night and, nine days later, didn't make the return trip—for a reason I still don't remember. I'd bombed two midterms, but I don't think that was it.

Nobody I'd met on campus phoned or emailed me the rest of the school year, save for Jeet, and one night in April, he called, ecstatic. His festival movie had won a prize and a little money, which he was using immediately to make a better version. He wanted me to come to Mississauga and work on it with him, and there was a spare room at his parents' house I could have rent-free, which sealed the deal. My folks, both high-school math teachers, had started charging me rent by then and I was working three nights a week at 7-Eleven just to pay them. The rest of the time I sat around the house with horror DVDs and novels I'd picked up at the library, dodging the constant question, "Shouldn't you be studying?", a not-so-gentle prod with the aim of getting me back to university or, at the very least, out of their house.

They didn't understand, though: I *was* studying. We made the movie, which in the end wasn't much better, and after that I started getting little jobs in the industry, usually in a crew with Jeet. I picked up forklift licences, my welding ticket, and a couple of reference letters before IATSE took me on.

That's kind of it, though. I've got a son who's seven, and a four-year-old daughter whose due date was a week after Hugh's moving day, plus a universal DVD player and hundreds of hard-to-find discs in languages I don't speak, some without subtitles even. It got out of control, and so did the empty beer cans that piled up on the coffee table every night. By the time Emily was born, Kate and I had stopped seeing each other between dinner and bed, and half the time I passed out on the couch anyway. At first, Kate would call *Goodnight* down the stairs after putting Cole to bed, but that stopped, too. I still thought about making my own movies, but by then it felt more like a dream, receding the way childhood does. It made me laugh, sometimes, when it didn't make me shudder.

Is that all, though? I drank too much, blew up my family temporarily, and now I just carry on one day at a time? Maybe. My life hasn't been very interesting outside this episode with Hugh I'm going to tell you about, which I'll remind you again involves a lot of dot-connecting on my part. It's the kind of story you can't hear first-hand unless you're suggestible, because all you'll want to do is poke holes in it. There's only so long you can listen to someone go on about being haunted.

I love horror stories, but myself, I don't believe in ghosts or possessions or any of it. And yet: the idea that something supernatural happened (or at least, in the mind of the person saying it happened, it happened) was too much to dismiss when the person happened to be Hugh. I was worried about him. From the facts I had, I needed to get the story together, and it seemed the best way was to just try telling it.

*

Hugh said he felt weird calling after so long—it really was a surprise—but also said I was the only person he knew who might have a pick-up truck, which I did. I muted my phone and asked Kate, who I didn't think would want me to go. It was getting harder for her to waddle around digging baby stuff out of closets and her mind was racing all the time about what we still had to do. She felt pretty sure, though, that the baby wouldn't come tonight and said I should take advantage, have a last night out in the city before a newborn took over our lives again. I wasn't about to argue. There'd be enough of that later.

On the phone, Hugh told me he'd been staying with Peter from work, the only one of his friends I've ever heard of, and Saturday would be the final day Christine would let him into the house to get the last of his things. It was also likely, he said, to be the last day before Chase moved in with her. Chase, who she'd screwed and then left Hugh for, some urban cowboy type who had around a hundred jobs—floorer, painter, landscaper and even, no help to us, mover. Christine had told Hugh not to worry about the drywall, as Chase was going to patch it, but Hugh asked me if I'd mind helping with it when I came. He wanted to do it himself because he had punched the hole. It was kind of a lot for the first phone call in years.

Hugh met me on the porch under a cloudy sky around eleven and I carried in my toolbox and power-sander, plus a tray with two extra-large coffees. He'd had a rough go lately, but at thirty, he was holding up alright. His dark hair hadn't receded like mine since I'd last seen him, and if he was overweight, I doubt it was by double digits. In the living room there was already a little pile of dust on the floor; he resumed rubbing his scrap of sandpaper on the big white bulge in the wall and said he was almost done, but he wasn't—he had used way too much mud. I plugged in my machine and ran it for a couple of minutes, brushed my hand over the smoothed spot and then pulled the plug. Hugh swept up, then I said, "Let's start loading. Dipshit can paint it for her."

There wasn't much to move—an old brown couch, a dresser and a few boxes—and once we were in the truck, Hugh read aloud as he wrote a text: *Ok, I'm gone.*

The new place wasn't far, up Bathurst to St. Clair then a little west to the side street where he'd live on the second floor of a sand-coloured, brick walk-up, built in the late forties. We brought the couch in last, twisting and tilting a few different ways up the stairs, and when we'd finished Hugh said, "Keep your shoes on"—the property manager had told him the building was sinking, meaning new nailheads were always poking up from the faded hardwood and intent on shredding socks.

I shrugged and said, "You just need a nail-set. I'd lend you mine, but I didn't bring it." Hugh gave me a puzzled look. I had forgotten how unmechanical he was. "You just hit it with a hammer, like a punch," I said. He nodded, but I don't think he knew what a punch was either, at least, not that kind.

Entering the apartment, you looked straight down a short hall into the bathroom, which I hoped Hugh would learn to close before inviting someone in. It wasn't so ugly, I just didn't think a cheap shower curtain and a toilet bowl in profile was the first impression he'd want to make. To the left was the galley kitchen and its twentieth-century appliances; to the right, the living room, with a lonely modem already connected in one corner. Beyond that was the bedroom. Every room except the bathroom was painted straw yellow, like an old hospital, and the battered floor sagged under the radiators along the exterior walls—but in all, the place looked pretty good, save for the boxes still everywhere.

I say 'still', but I'm not sure how long it had been since Peter had lent Hugh his car to move them in and pick up the rickety bed frame from Craigslist that I bolted together with my drill. Hugh laid a thin, faded, blue futon on top and I slapped it.

"*This*," I said, "is where the magic is going to happen."

Hugh threw back a weak, "Fuck off," but he was laughing—holding it in a bit, like he'd forgotten how, but finally laughing.

*

We'd put a twelve-pack in the fridge and it was cold now. I parked the truck for the night, and when the beers were gone, we walked to St. Clair to find a bar that served dinner. The only one we saw was at Bathurst, the Sycamore Tavern—*the Syc*, I overheard someone waiting for someone else yell into his phone over loud nineties rock when we entered. A hot, young blonde brought us nachos and burgers, plus a whole bunch more beers, and when I'd heard enough about Christine—Hugh'd been going for a while—I finally said, "On the bright side, now you can bang somebody else." He started to object but I added, "You could even bang our waitress." He looked uncomfortable and said he couldn't. I said again that he could. I'm not proud of it now—drunk generally, as well as presently, the last thing he should've been doing was starting a new relationship—but when she came back with another round of beers, I introduced him.

"Hi, Hugh," she replied stiffly.

"He's new in the neighbourhood," I said. "And newly single. This being the closest bar to his apartment, you'll get sick of his ugly face."

Hugh put his head into his hands. I was busting his balls, but I think I offended him. His acne was long gone, and hadn't even been that bad, but his face had always been a sore point. I had kind of forgotten.

Hugh mumbled, "I don't even know what to say."

Well, that was fun.

"I just thought you should know each other's names," I said.

The waitress had been pleasant before I'd opened my mouth—flustered by the busy Saturday night, maybe, but pleasant—and now her smile was back, like a threat had passed.

"Kelly," she said. And then she walked away.

Hugh said, "Thanks, man, now I've got to find a new bar. Any time I come in she's going to think I'm trying to hook up with her."

"Just see what happens."

We drank the last round so slowly that when Kelly returned to offer us last call, we still had beer left. I couldn't finish mine and Hugh probably shouldn't have drained his. He slurred a little and insisted on paying, saying at least three times, "Thank you so much for coming to help me." He keyed his PIN into the machine then gave it back to Kelly without looking up.

"See you soon, Hugh," she said. Her smile seemed less automatic now.

I said, "Get her number," louder than I thought I did.

Hugh stared at me, his mouth open a little. He looked at Kelly and said, "Uh…"

"Is that yours?"

He didn't start nodding before she had picked up his phone and started typing. I wasn't surprised that he hadn't set a lock on it.

"Four-three-seven?" he said when she handed it back.

"Yeah, I guess they're out of six-four-sevens."

"Remember when there was only four-one-six?" I asked.

"No," she said.

Ignoring me—good decision—Hugh said to her with a little smile, "I'll call anyway." I couldn't believe it. He was out of his tree, but that was actually smooth.

She said, "You'd better," then walked away toward the taps, where a bartender with a close-shaved head waited with a dirty look for her. We stood up, Hugh trying not to blare a shit-eating grin, and together we wobbled toward the door.

SUNDAY

HUGH GASPS FOR AIR. He's flat on his back and doesn't know where he is. The woman atop him a moment ago is gone and so is the black hair that hung in front of her face, tresses so long he's sure he felt them brush his torso. Inside his boxers he's wet and sticky, still throbbing. Heart still pounding.

Fog hangs in his brain, bitter taste in his mouth. First light slips between the threadbare curtains and his eyes adjust. He recognizes the stack of boxes, the dresser cockeyed in the corner: his new bedroom as we left it yesterday afternoon. A cold dribble runs down his thigh and he thinks of the tissues on the side table before remembering there are none. There's no side table. Christine kept the side tables.

He tries to sit up, but can't.

Tries bringing a hand to his chest.

The hand doesn't move.

Breath comes short and shallow. He strains to roll to his side but his core is pinned—like she's still on him, but not at all fun. Brain flashes *Kick!* to his right leg but no response. The pressure's on his whole body, *in* his body, holding him down by his bone marrow.

A fine layer of sweat chills him.

A cry rises in his throat, but no sound comes.

He shifts his thoughts back to his hand, its pinkie and the pad on its tip. If he can just move this one… he visualizes it separating from the fitted sheet and feels pain in his teeth, like they're grinding, though they don't move either—not until a tiny muscle wakes in the finger and frees itself reluctantly, like Velcro. He hears the ripping sound in his mind and the groan that escapes his lips.

His chest loosens as he breathes out, then tests the finger, raising it but not daring to touch it down in case it sticks again. Rolling the motion into the rest of the hand, he brings the ring, middle and index to life, one at a time, in a timid piano warmup. The left hand comes back online even faster. He tries his big toe next and the whole foot moves with it.

His limbs all function now, but he stays on his back a moment, breathing in the nose, out the mouth, and letting his heart slow. How long was he frozen there? Two minutes? Three? It felt longer. He shifts his shoulders a little, then moves his hips and feels another cold dribble on his groin. He mutters, "Shit," and rises unsteadily from the bed to go clean himself. His head aches and his stomach burbles beer remnants as he pulls on yesterday's jeans, gently opens the door, then treads softly across the living room so as not to wake me.

*

My phone alarm rang a few minutes after he went back to bed. "Up at six-thirty, on the road by seven," I had said as I lay down on the couch, and though it was harder than expected—hangovers got harder every time—I was sitting up, dressed and fiddling with my phone, which said 6:51. Hugh's voice from the bedroom asked, "Are you alright to drive?"

As the first words of the morning, these might have sounded to some like, *How soon will you be getting lost?*, but I don't think he wanted me to leave. I know he cared about me, too. His eyes told me when he opened the door and they went straight to my feet, which were already in my steel-toes.

"You in a hurry?"

"Nah," I said. "Well, maybe. I told Kate I'd do a bunch of shit—and I guess the baby could come, who knows, right?"

"Right." He looked again at my boots.

"The nails are bad," I said. "I caught one on my way to piss."

"Just now?"

"Half an hour ago, maybe—"

"Did you hear me get up?"

He sounded embarrassed to ask, but I hadn't so I said, "No." My head was splitting. "You got an aspirin?" I asked.

He shuffled to the bathroom, where I heard him rummage in a couple of boxes before he met me in the little hallway with a bottle of ibuprofen. I squeezed past him into the kitchen where I put my mouth beneath the faucet.

"Want to go for breakfast?" he asked.

I wiped my lips with my fingers. "I should get going. I'll hit a Tim's or something."

"Okay." He looked concerned. "Take your time there. And eat a lot."

Something made him flinch then, and he reached for the pocket of his jeans.

I felt my grin. "Kelly!"

He looked up from his phone and said, "Nothing, actually. I don't know what that was."

"You have to call her, though."

"She was kidding," he said. "Four-three-seven? That's a fake number."

"No, it's real. I read about it in the paper."

"Why do you remember that?"

"I don't know." We laughed, but we couldn't prevent the silence that followed. I glanced around the room for anything I might have forgotten, patting each of my pockets once—*keys, phone, wallet*—then said again that I should go.

"I'll walk you out." He stepped barefoot into his sneakers then turned the bolt. The chain latch rattled when he opened the door.

I hadn't noticed the day before how brown the hall was: brown carpet, walls browned with dirt that no longer washed off and old sconces casting brownish light all the way to the lobby, where one mirrored wall stood at the foot of the stairs opposite a bank of mailboxes numbered up to 24 and framed by wood with a dark finish. We went out to my truck, three spaces over from the building's front walk.

"So, that way?" I asked, pointing east toward similar apartments I could see from here. "Then right, right again on St. Clair to…"

"Dufferin. Or Keele, I guess, to the Gardiner." He paused. "St. Clair's a lot slower since they built the streetcar, though, so you could go left first, to Oakwood and Eglinton, then west to 401, 427, 403." I think he knew he was rambling. "But there's construction on Eg, they're digging the new subway—well, not subway, underground light rail, but because of that there might be *less* traffic, especially because it's early on a Sunday, so maybe it's fine after all…"

He definitely didn't want me to leave. On the phone, in the truck, at the bar, and now as well: he seemed lonely. I wondered again whether he had other friends to talk to, but I had to go. I opened the door and cranked the window down before I got in—the truck's a real treasure, one of the last you could get with no power anything.

"Will you be alright?"

I looked hard at his eyes and asked back, "Will you?"

"Yeah," Hugh said. "Of course. Just going to unpack today."

"Get the place the way you want it as fast as you can. And unpack your TV last, so you don't just sit around instead of—*Whoa*."

"What?" He started turning his head.

"No, don't look!" I lowered my voice. "Your neighbour is smokin' hot—she's fit, she's younger than you… she's got *really* long hair…"

He made to turn again.

"I said *don't*—"

"Dark hair?"

A bit specific, but I don't know, maybe that was his new thing.

"Yeah—"

"Like, brown? Or black?"

"Do you care that much?"

He did. He seemed shaken.

"You'll know when you see her," I said.

"What's she doing?"

"Just standing there. You know, I think she's looking at me, actually."

"Bullshit."

I started the engine. "See how it goes. And call the waitress."

He stretched through the window for a handshake that worked out more like a low-five then mumbled, "Thanks for everything." It was hard to see him so down, especially after so long without seeing him at all, but I suppose he'd been through a lot. People change, too. They come back into your life, you say it's good to see them, and when it's over you realize you don't know them anymore and you're not sure it was.

I may have been more optimistic then, more than four years ago, when I put the truck into gear and said, "Give me a call in a day or two," but even as I stepped off the brake I wasn't sure I'd pick up. I felt like I was abandoning him, but also like he wanted me to— like it was time to put the B-story down and let the protagonist get to it on his own.

*

Hugh stares up the street a few seconds after I disappear around the corner, then turning to face his building again, notices the shadows on the window ledges; black diagonals drawn down its face. In weather clearer than yesterday's, it's more imposing, almost shocking against a blue sky.

He also notices no woman outside. A smile climbs his cheeks and he calls me *fucker* in his head. *There probably never was.* He enters the building and starts up the stairs, arranging the keys on his ring in the order he'll use them, outside door, mailbox, Apartment Ten. A few envelope corners stick out under the door before his own and he thinks, *The neighbour's on vacation,* which is just as well; he's too hungover to make small-talk.

In his living room, he surveys his scattered belongings and the boxes stacked beside the window. The bent venetian blinds have been left open. Beneath the sill and the radiator that looks hastily painted white, he sees how badly the floor droops. Before now, he's lived in his parents' home, and a shared dorm room, and a filthy house where he and four other students split the rent, and then the place with Christine—he's thirty, and he's never lived alone.

He needs to open more boxes before work resumes tomorrow, but the headache is tightening around his brain. He bolts the apartment door and latches the chain, which rattles again. Had someone left this morning, he'd have heard her—*heard them,* he corrects himself, it's a hypothetical person. He blinks twice and shakes his head then walks to the bathroom, telling himself there was no woman. The Advil he dug out earlier is in the medicine cabinet now. He takes two, bending under the faucet to wash them down, then peels off his shirt and goes back to bed.

*

Her lips shine red and part as she moans from deeper than her throat; a sound that vibrates under Hugh's skin while he lies on his back with his eyes wide, wet with sweat as the window smelts midday sunlight. Hands with long fingernails pin his chest, but the pressure is on his throat—lungs burning, windpipe sealing off, head spinning from lack of oxygen and toward exhilarating blackout as she takes him in deeper, as he grows harder inside her and the flimsy bed cries like it's tearing apart. The wood slats heave a final complaint as he comes violently and she lands heavily on his chest.

She lies there a time, breasts pressed against him, and though Hugh wants nothing other than to wrap her in his arms and hold her there, he already knows: he can't. His breathing slows, and when his nerves wake enough to feel the tickle of her long, black hair on his cheek, he swings both arms up fast to encircle her before she can get away.

His hands land on his opposite shoulders, though, and with the slight slapping sound she's disappeared again.

*

When next he wakes, he feels more tired than before. His headache hasn't resolved. He checks the time on his phone, *12:36.* In his mind he sings, *Morning comes twice a day, or not at all,* some old, alt-country song about drinking. (Are there any about anything else?) His stomach gurgles and he hurries to the toilet where he bends over, sure he's going to throw up, but the feeling passes. He straightens up and leans his back against the cool wall tiles. His balls ache, his cock feels swollen and his chest hurts, too. He looks at the mould-stained ceiling and exhales, then as he lowers his head, glimpses himself in the mirror.

A red streak runs from one shoulder diagonally to his belly.

He didn't dream her, and she hurt him.

Where did she go?

He flings open the bathroom door and sees from there that the main deadbolt is horizontal—locked from inside or with a key—and the chain latch is still in place. He checks the living room window then the one in the bedroom. Both are locked from the inside. She must have left as quietly as she came in; he didn't hear the bedroom door or footsteps, a post-sex pee, a flushing toilet, nothing. She could have gone home, though, if she lives close by, especially if she lives in the same building, but then how did she lock—

She *who*, though?

Hadn't I been putting him on? There wasn't any dark-haired woman standing outside, he tells himself—and if she were in the apartment, she'd have nowhere to hide.

So how did she get out?

Feeling ridiculous, he tries the windows again and finds them locked as they were a moment ago. He crosses the hall next, the first time he's entered the kitchen since the showing with the property manager, Nick. He doesn't remember it being so small—he can reach the fridge on his left from the hall, and did a few times to get beer last night, alternating turns with me.

He also doesn't recall the door straight ahead of him. He's sure he didn't open it during the viewing like he did the closets in the bedroom and living room, and though I was only there the one night, I don't remember seeing it, either. I'd have made a crack about *Rosemary's Baby* and Hugh'd have met it with a blank stare. *Is it a pantry…?* He grips the knob, splattered with the yellow paint that was slapped on the walls and trim ages ago, but it doesn't turn. The paint was applied so badly that some dried between the frame and door, and it hasn't split. The door clearly hasn't opened in years.

He dreamed the woman, he decides.

He must have.

It's rare for him, though—he wakes from a dream maybe five times a year, and when he tries to remember what was so vivid a minute or two previous, he finds it already gone.

So what happened to give him the same, unshakeable dream twice in a row?

Lots.

His move-out is finished and so are he and Christine, finally and for-real this time.

It was his first night in a new bed—and a whole new apartment.

He ate too many nachos. Drank far too much beer.

He met Kelly.

And this morning, I told him I saw a dark-haired woman outside.

He then recalls the blue cover of his condensed *Interpretation of Dreams*; a cheap, battered copy of which he read at least a part in first-year psychology before he decided a diploma in graphic design would be more useful. He types *Frued* into the search box on his phone and, after his spelling is autocorrected, he relearns the list of defense mechanisms. Faced with upheaval lately, his subconscious is protecting itself: Christine, a blonde, is a recent source of pain, so when he encounters another blonde infatuation in Kelly, his desire to be aggressively fucked by her—a specific desire he doesn't know he has, but concedes he probably does—manifests in a dark-haired monster.

He laughs to himself. If psych were so easy, how'd he manage only a C? It wasn't his worst grade, but wasn't far from his best, either. He didn't apply himself, he supposes. College is a boozy blur now, the first year especially, and like the period last night between eating dinner and getting Kelly's number, more than one block of a few hours is missing. The drinking must have something to do with the dreams, but still: next time he speaks to Nick, he'll ask where the door leads.

His roiling stomach has finally settled and he's hungry. It's one o'clock and he hasn't eaten today. He opens the fridge, forgetting he hasn't gone shopping yet, then shuts it again when he finds it empty. He goes to the entrance and puts on his shoes.

He just got into this apartment, but already getting out feels like a good idea.

*

The Syc's the only spot that's not a chain offering oily subs or rubbery pizza, greasy burgers or ham and egg on your choice of pastry. In front, the sandwich board reads *BRUNCH* in flowery letters and Hugh wonders if Kelly drew them, if she has a creative side. Maybe they'll talk shop about negative space. As she closed last night, she won't be working this morning, will she? He thinks better of checking and chooses the coffee chain. He doesn't want to seem like a stalker—and do people still do the three-day rule? He's only heard of it, never done it. He's only ever dated Christine, and it's different when you meet in your dorm.

He scarfs an egg on a croissant with ham and Swiss, and when he leaves holding a coffee still too hot to drink, he tries a different route home, north along Bathurst. It's a big street, but mostly lined with low-rise apartments like his, and quiet, apart from the one number-seven bus that whooshes past. He doesn't know there's no east-west road before the gas station well beyond his street, and when he finally reaches the boulevard, he pauses before walking through its gate. It seems unfinished, which it is; I've looked up all kinds of things about his neighbourhood. The guy who built Casa Loma planned to house his workers on this street but ran out of money. Hugh doesn't know this, or that before the massive bridge was built over the ravine he doesn't know is called Cedarvale, Ernest Hemingway lived a few steps up Bathurst—he's just looking for the best street to follow home. He passes two and arrives at a cul-de-sac surrounding a grass circle, after which he comes to an older, smaller bridge made of wood and for pedestrians only.

To his left he sees Vaughan Road, which should take him home, but with nowhere else to be, he shrugs and walks to the sunny centre of the structure, passing the *Glen Cedar Bridge* plaque without reading it. He stops to lean his forearms over the black metal railing and lets his eyes scan the path under him, following anything that moves out of sight past the treetops in the distance: bicycles lazy and racing, families meandering, dogs leashed and not, and joggers. So many joggers.

Somewhere in his apartment, there's a pair of shoes, hardly used since he was the last cut from the cross-country team in college. He searches his memory for when or how he gave it up, but can't recall a specific moment or conscious choice. The last run he remembers was with Christine, and it was long enough ago that he could still set any pace—all of which were too fast for her. She seemed to like the idea of running much more than actually doing it; she wouldn't run without him, but the few times they went together, she complained that he took it too seriously. At some point, he must have absorbed the idea that if she didn't enjoy something then he couldn't either. It feels pretty stupid now.

More runners pass: some in couples going the same pace and some solo, some straining and red-faced in beer-case, freebie T-shirts while others sail, deep in focus, setting new personal bests, training for marathons or halves, distances Hugh didn't try before quitting. He stares into the distance a moment longer and thinks,

Maybe, then steps back from the railing to find his way home.

*

There aren't days left in the weekend now, just hours, and Hugh hasn't unpacked much more than the particle-board coffee table he ordered online—an assembly job even he could figure out, six pieces shrink-wrapped with a tiny bag of supports for its cardboard bottom shelf. He centres it in front of the ratty, brown couch Christine had hated since he claimed it curbside on Free Furniture Day, the last day of term when all the students leave; the couch he granted asylum in the previous house's basement as part of a never-achieved man-cave; the couch he slept on for two miserable months before she concluded yes, she wanted him out.

He exhales and lifts a box from the stack beside the radiator down to the coffee table. If he doesn't start now the stack will stay there all week, as will the various bags to empty and piles to sort. He hasn't recognized the warp in the cardboard nor its slight musty smell, so when he opens the flaps and reaches in, he's surprised to brush up against a well-worn fleece. He smiles. Of course he's opened this box first, the least relevant one, full of things he can't throw out but has no use for either—a time-capsule that stayed in the basement corner beside the old couch, largely untouched since he moved in with Christine. He pulls out his dorm hoodie and carefully unrolls it, recalling what he wrapped inside years ago, a *Nightmare on Elm Street* pint glass I'd brought him back from Universal Studios in Florida. It was my favourite movie as a kid, but Hugh was always too scared to watch it with me. The cartoony versions of Johnny Depp as a teenager and Robert Englund as Freddy Kreuger stare back at him and he realizes two things: he never did watch it, and the glass is now the only one he owns. His disparate plates, bowls and silverware, unpacked the day he moved in with Christine, had gone right back into their box, and the next morning she'd gone shopping. The sets she unloaded from the cab that afternoon were still in the house and fully hers now.

He reaches back into the carton, and near the bottom his fingers bump the jangling wooden box that stores his high school running medals: two silvers, a gold, and a dozen bronzes. Jake Latos, Muhammed Abiz, Hugh Campbell—everyone knew the finishing order before each race started. One silver came in a race Latos sat out, and the other when Abiz tripped and didn't finish, but for the gold Hugh had simply beaten them, just had a day where everything went right.

His shoes are under the medal box, and though they aren't pristine like he remembered, they look to still have some clicks in them. He remembers writing the purchase date inside with a black marker so he'd know when to replace them.

He peels back the insole.

Apr 2007

Nine and a half years.

He stands and takes the shoes to the entranceway, where he won't forget about them again.

*

If you feel like I'm breaking off abruptly, or arbitrarily, don't worry. I feel it, too. But on the other hand, I don't need to tell you Hugh opened a few more boxes, hooked up his TV like I told him not to, bought groceries (including a microwave dinner he ate when he got home) and then went to bed—and if all this is inference anyway, you can infer it yourself, right?

I've seen it countless times in the movies I've worked on: we spend a couple of days filming these introspective scenes, set to sombre music, where people shuffle around the house or go running, and in the end, they get hacked together into a montage, or better, cut entirely. I'm skipping over everything I can, and trying not to be cliché, but I'm not making a movie—I'm just trying to get Hugh's story together, to reconstruct what was in his head as best I can.

You may find too little wound up on the cutting room floor. Or maybe too many scenes start with him waking up.

MONDAY

HIS EYES SPRING OPEN. It's dark, but a lamp is on. His neck hurts, oddly curved over the arm of the couch, and there's weight on his torso—but less this time. He backs his chin up and sees the start-your-own-business book he's been reading for months, tented on his chest. Christine bought it for him the year before, and said it might inspire him to do something with his life, but all it's done so far is make him want to sleep. He squints and finds his phone on the coffee table beside his dinner's cardboard tray and congealing remains.

It's 4:21 a.m.

He didn't mean to sleep here. He had gone to bed earlier, after inspecting the windows and confirming the main door was bolted and latched, but on the cracked ceiling a shadow moved like a snake when headlights passed and he couldn't stop seeing it when he closed his eyes. Traffic slowed after a while but then, with the city's accumulated daytime noise gone for the night, he began hearing the bleat in his fridge motor—a worn belt, probably, though I can tell you he wouldn't have known that. He fixated on the rhythm, unsure why until lyrics followed in his head.

Oh my little pretty one, pretty one, when you gonna gimme some time, Sharona… oh, you make my motor run…

What was the next line? He was drumming one hand on his thigh and the other on the ratty mattress before he stopped himself. It was the cheesiest old song. But in the dark and alone, he admitted sleep wasn't coming. He took his phone from the floor beside the bed and looked up the lyrics.

Never gonna stop, give it up, always such a dirty mind, always get it up, for the touch of the younger kind…

It wasn't just cheesy, it was kind of gross—like he'd be if he called Kelly, he thought, glad to have no intention of doing so. There was no way he was what she wanted, not at her age (which he still didn't know, though she was clearly younger), and with her big green eyes and another decent pair, she could pull in any man she wanted. And say she did want someone older: plenty were better-looking (sorry, buddy), had travelled to more countries—Hugh'd been to four, if the States counted— and they held more interesting jobs, read more books, remembered to vote. Made more money. They drove cars that cost more than his parents' house and could essentially wave a wand to make sure she never had to enter a bar like the Syc again. He was describing enough men *younger* than himself, too—and the older he got, the more there would be. It was like Peter had warned a few performance reviews ago: if you're not moving forward, you're going backward.

She had given him her number, though, hadn't she?

He looked in his contacts—yes—and was reassured to separate a real incident from a dream.

More headlights passed his window and the crack in the ceiling slithered again, a long black hair in a swimming pool.

With a chill he knew why he couldn't sleep. His chest hurt thinking about it. But had the woman really left marks? The image fixed in his memory was a broad, deep slice, already cauterized on a wide, bare patch of his chest. He told himself she couldn't have then got up and walked to the bathroom, where he turned on the light.

Not even his chest hair was disturbed.

So had he dreamed this, too?

Restless, he resumed unpacking, and soon discovered the box containing the few bottles of liquor he owned. He didn't normally drink spirits, didn't remember how he'd come to own most of them, but thinking it would help him sleep he sipped an Irish whiskey from his one, well over-sized glass, served neat because he didn't have ice trays.

Not knowing what else to do, he took the glass and the book unearthed earlier that evening to the couch and lay down, where he apparently fell asleep.

He fills the glass with water in the kitchen now and will try again to go to bed. He turns off the lamp in the living room, then in the dark promptly snags his sock on a nailhead. He feels the hole as wide as his thumb when he frees the fibre, and relief at having torn clothing and not flesh.

In the bedroom, he lies down and pulls the blankets over himself. He closes his eyes. The fridge bleats. His mind roams some more, listing what he'll unpack when he comes home from work, counting items already pulled from boxes and others he still needs to find.

It's nearly six when his thoughts circle back to his running shoes. It's still dark, but birds have begun to sing.

I'm not sleeping anyway.

He rises from the bed and takes shorts and a beer-case giveaway T-shirt from the dresser. The insoles are soft, the still-supple tongue forms to his foot as he tightens the laces, and after raising and kicking each leg a couple of times, he pricks sound buds into his ears, steps

into the hall and locks his door behind him. He descends
the stairs, then the stoop, then takes his first quickened
stride. His ankles ache as they spring off the ground
faster than he's asked them to in a long time, but after
fumbling to press Play and put his phone in his pocket,
it's like he never quit: *Highway to Hell* still sounds like
starting out, and the driving drums and crashing guitars
won't let up for thirty-five minutes, not until *Love Hungry
Man* ends.

Thirty-five—it was a time he had obsessed over,
nowhere near the ten-k world record but good enough
to win his age group most days, and he'd wanted to just
once cross this imagined finish line, if not a real one, with
the tempo still high in his ears, adrenaline in the red, not
thinking of anything, not feeling his feet anymore, just
flying. Before he made the distance, though, every time,
the lazy closer *Night Prowler* would start and remind him
again to get faster, dragging on until the tape would
auto-reverse and relaunch into the title track of little use
by the time he was cooling down.

Today he crests breathing walls he remembers
well—five minutes, twelve, twenty-five—and the next
one is thirty-seven. He won't get ten k today, not even
close, but he finds his wind on backstreets that take him
to Eglinton and discovers the north entrance to the
ravine. Past the park, on the gravel path lined by reeds
and cattails, is a tall wooden staircase to a bridge that

must be the one he stopped on yesterday. Bon Scott whines, *Watch out tonight, when you turn out the light, 'cause I'm your niiiight prowler* and Hugh's flagging like the tempo. He speeds up to chase the familiar consolation prize—covering the most ground he can before the album ends—and recalls his high-school training, up and down hills while the lactic acid cried in his calves. His machine-gun steps echo into the woods as he charges to the top of the stairs then slows to a walk, chest heaving. The album's ended and, in the digital version, he prefers silence to the clunk of a tape changing directions. The sky's much lighter now and from the bridge he sees the trees have started to turn orange. He takes in a deep breath through his nose.

Before he can exhale, his shoulders and chest tighten.

His steps waver.

His legs give out and he falls on his back.

His head strikes the wooden surface.

The woman descends on him, vermilion lips shining on her pale face as she reveals teeth, sharp in her smile. She stares with eyes now turning red.

This is it, he thinks. *This is how I die.*

The eyes bore deep into him—

*

He wakes with a start, on his back, in his bed. His legs are tender and the bottoms of his feet raw. Above his left eye, he has a headache for the ages. He fumbles for his phone, but it's not near the bed. He feels the sheets on his skin and realizes he's naked, but doesn't remember taking off his running clothes, doesn't remember anything since the bridge. The T-shirt's nowhere in sight, but the shorts are on the floor, spilling earbuds out the pocket. At the end of the wire, he retrieves his phone, which shows 9:40. He's late for work. He texts Peter then hustles to the shower.

He's never late, and never goes to work without having breakfast first. After skulking in around ten-thirty, garnering a little wave from Peter when he does, he lasts fifteen minutes before taking the elevator back down to the Tim Hortons in the lobby. Two straight days, two straight ham-and-egg sandwich breakfasts; it wouldn't bother me, but Hugh still feels guilt for eating processed meat, guilt given to him by, yeah, you guessed who.

The line-up is long and Hugh drifts in thought until a "NEXT!" from behind the counter shakes him, too loud to not be a third or fourth attempt. Feeling the scowls behind him, he sheepishly orders, pays and moves toward the pick-up counter, looking again at what distracted him—a woman a few places ahead of him in a mid-length navy-blue dress, playing with a strand of long, dark hair, and the massive blue stone on her finger framed in a square of maybe twenty tiny diamonds. Her posture is confident and Hugh's anxious to meet her eyes, to get a read: did she just buy this air of strength and shit-togetherness, or is the person underneath happy?

While his sandwich is readied, he tries to look at his receipt and order number instead of staring, but can't keep his eyes off the black hair that hides her ears and falls nearly to her ass. He comes closest to seeing her face when he discerns the movement of her jaw, saying *Thank you* as she pays and collects her yogurt with the hand that leaves behind a final, bright blue and white sparkle of a class he'll never afford. Hugh was the guy who, walking through the Bay a few years ago, thought himself subtle when he asked Christine in the jewellery section, "What styles do you like, just generally," smiling a little and aware he was tipping his hand.

"Just generally, you should pick a better store," she replied.

No compromise, no hesitation, and no more talk about getting married. How stupid he was to think she'd come around when all the serious conversations trended the other way, toward how inadequate, unsatisfactory, disappointing he was, and always more deficiencies she was adamant he'd never overcome.

When did I start believing her?

It's time to start over. It's okay to start over. He should be with a woman who looks like the one in the blue dress—not just physically, not necessarily physically at all, but someone who looks like she feels that good.

Someone who feels good about being with him. He thinks of Kelly as he calls the elevator and admits I was right: he has to try, and so what if it proves as futile as pursuing the engaged and clearly happy woman in the blue dress, or the other one, who attacked him this morning—

The one who doesn't exist, he reminds himself. But then, what happened on the bridge? It's no easier to believe, but he's less sure he dreamed her now that she's also stalked him outdoors, overpowered him and abducted him—if being dragged home can be called an abduction. And is *dragged* even the right word? He woke with the usual headache, but no new cuts or scrapes—so did she carry him? He knows she's strong from the way she held him down in bed…

In the elevator he texts:

Did you see or hear anyone else in the apartment yesterday morning?

I wouldn't normally use my phone outside of lunch, when my hands are free and clean, but there was so much going on then. Emily could've been born any minute. But as I'd checked now, I wrote back, *Like who?*

Bing. *A girl sneaking out?*

You sure as hell didn't get that waitress home, I typed, feeling a goofy smile invading my face as I added, *How drunk *were* you?* and sent.

Hugh writes back, *Forget it. I had a dream I guess.*

He re-enters his office suite, turning off his phone as well as thoughts of dark-haired women. Whether or not he's losing his mind, almost half the day is gone and he still hasn't done any work.

The most recent message in his inbox is from Peter and entirely in the subject line: *Leafs game tonight!!!!!* He doesn't reply—Peter will come by his desk soon enough to make sure they're still on—and moves to the next email down, the week's list of sale items. He opens it then begins trying to concentrate, gathering images of steak, pumpkins, toilet paper and more for next week's flyer.

*

Peter appears again at five o'clock exactly. There's no rush to get to the bar, no competition for tables in the dim room with the pitcher and half-price wings combo below the building adjacent to theirs, accessible via an underground path without ever going outside—and yet, they never delay in getting there and putting down a couple of pints before the game starts.

Once they've been seated and each has ordered the special, Hugh with his pitcher delayed until they've finished one, Peter says, "I'm sorry for not helping Saturday." His grandparents in Sweden were celebrating their anniversary and he had to video call with his wife and kids.

"Are you kidding?" Hugh says. "You've already helped so much."

Three weeks ago, he'd awkwardly closed Peter's office door intending only to ask for schedule flexibility to look at apartments but wound up explaining everything about the break-up. "You're still living together?" Peter asked, and when Hugh confirmed, Peter insisted he come stay in his basement, starting that night. It was risky to rely personally on his manager and he tried feebly to decline, but it was exactly the offer he needed. He couldn't live another day with Christine—or even at the house without her, had she briefly moved out, which she wouldn't have, or if she had, she wouldn't have *stayed* out, she would've kept bursting in like a band of thunderstorms and berating him about why the relationship wasn't working—"*Didn't* work," he'd have corrected, "you broke up with me"—then stomping out again to her parents' place or, if he were honest with himself, to Chase's, probably.

The bar's far from full but a couple of big voices among some suit-wearing MBA types and jersey-sporting students occupy the space. Peter not-so-discreetly points to the young people, four of five of them male. "If you're looking, there's the only woman in the place who doesn't work here—in the pink jersey, pretending she'd rather be friends with men than women while secretly sleeping with one of the guys she's here with." Hugh doesn't think she has to be, but looks anyway as Peter asks, "Which one do you think it is?"

"Maybe she's really a fan," Hugh says.

Peter laughs loudly.

The server returns with the first pitcher and Peter gives her the up-and-down-the-elevator look. She's wearing the customary, uncomfortable-looking short skirt, low-neck top, push-up bra with visible straps and the highest heels, all of it black. He stares at her ass as she walks away then says, "You should try with her."

Hugh reaches for the pitcher. "What is it with servers?" he asks, shaking his head as though I didn't get him Kelly's number two nights before. He fills Peter's glass then his own and says, "They're paid to be nice to us."

"A man's never had a problem a waitress couldn't solve," Peter says, raising his pint. "If you don't get laid, you'll at least get drunk."

Hugh says nothing, but cursorily clinks his glass. They see a lot of each other, but they aren't close, and he feels the distance at the start of these evenings before the beer loosens them up. The suit-wearers' volume rises as two get obnoxious debating which trade was the Leafs' worst. *Long list*, Hugh thinks, staring through the screen and not even watching. He was a child the last time he truly believed, and since then he's seen so much mismanagement and simply bad hockey that he's not sure he even likes the sport anymore.

"Are you okay?"

It doesn't sound like Peter's first attempt to get his attention. Hugh says, "Yeah." He feels his face being studied.

"You were late this morning," Peter says. "And you look like shit."

"Thanks, man."

"Is there something you want to talk about?"

An imaginary woman is fucking me to death.

"New place," Hugh says. "It's been hard to get to sleep."

"You probably just need to get laid."

"I actually think I should take some time on my own. I mean, nine years, that's a long—"

"No way," Peter says. "I love Laura, I love my kids, but if I had my old life back I'd be out crushing it, all the fucking time." He's good-looking, a former U.S. college player—his dad played hockey, too, that's why he left Sweden—and when Laura turned out to be Canadian, she moved him here. "Do you remember when we were like twenty-one, and all the women our age we wanted were with grown-up men?" he continues. "We're the men, now." Hugh rolls his eyes. The Bruins score but Peter keeps talking without noticing: "…you have a good job. You don't live with your parents or have roommates. And younger men are so insecure, always having existential crises—"

"Who says I'm not having an existential crisis?"

"You may be! You just don't tell women anymore—"

Hugh sighs and asks, "How do I get to know someone, just out of nowhere…"

Peter doesn't seem to hear the question.

"—you're mature, you're a man. You lucky bastard." Peter's glass is already empty. He exhales through his nose, shaking his head a little. "They're going to come to you now."

Hugh can't hide his smile.

"What is it?" Peter asks. He signals the server for the second pitcher.

"It's nothing."

"My baby doesn't sleep and we're done having kids." He points at his lap. "End of the road for this guy. Tell me *everything*."

"Sorry to get your hopes up," Hugh says. "It's just a phone number… and probably fake."

"Yes, women give out fake phone numbers all the time."

Hugh doesn't buy the sarcasm. "If I looked like her, I'd have to," he says.

The other tables erupt in a cheer. The Leafs have scored. Peter stands up and whoops and claps his hands, egging on the loudest of the other patrons. He seems to have a buzz and Hugh feels his own starting. Red beams over the room from a novelty oscillating goal light. Hugh looks up at the replay. It's an ugly goal from a cluster of bodies in front of the net.

"So when was this?" Peter asks when play resumes.

"Saturday."

"Have you done anything yet?"

"No."

"Do you *want* to try with her?" Peter asks.

"I think so."

"So send her a text."

Hugh met Christine before he bought his first cell phone, and hasn't heard of apps that let you meet dates by swiping right or left on a photo.

"I could invite her over for dinner," he says. "Buy all my kitchen stuff and get set up—"

"That's too much," Peter says. "Go slow."

"Ask her to get a drink, maybe?"

"*Maybe* is the best part—just play it cool."

Hugh takes his phone from his pocket. "Hi," he reads aloud as he types. "Would, you, like, to, get, a—"

Peter slaps Hugh's hand. "What did I just say?"

Hugh creases his forehead. He doesn't get it yet.

"Work up to it a little. Say you've been busy at work, or moving in, whatever. But don't let her know how much you want this. See if *she* wants this."

"And what if she doesn't?"

"Then you let it go."

Hey! Sorry, been busy at work and unpacking. What's up?

He shows Peter the screen for inspection.

"Maybe tell her who it is?"

"Right." He laughs. "Right." He adds *(It's Hugh)* to the end and asks, "Good?"

"Good."

"Maybe a smiley?"

"If you must."

Colon, close-parenthesis. Send. Hugh exhales, realizing he's been holding his breath. He feels wetness in his armpits and is sure Peter can see it on his shirt.

The phone vibrates. They exchange a look.

Hugh reads aloud: "*So do you want to do something?*"

"She wants this," Peter says.

"Okay, wise one," Hugh says. "What do I do next? Ask when?"

Peter shakes his head. "Make a bid—be confident and pick a night, see if she takes it."

Hugh types, *I'm free tomorrow*, and sets the phone on the table so Peter can review it.

"Sure. Send."

"It's not too soon?"

"If the three-day rule's a thing, it's already shot."

Hugh sends.

The phone buzzes again.

Mon and Tue r my only nights off

Again.

Or catch me after work one night

Again.

Whenever ur free

"Where does she work?" Peter asks.

"The bar around the corner from my place. The Sycamore."

"Oh."

"What?"

"You don't want to foul the nest."

"I know." A groan moves through the room, Boston has retaken the lead. "I should have mentioned that before we texted her."

Peter shrugs. "Just don't show up before she finishes her shift—and for god's sake, don't hang out there, take her somewhere else."

They drain their pints and look immediately for the server. Another, bigger groan: Boston again, 3-1 now. Hugh feels the previous beers rising to his head before the next pitcher arrives and, as has been the trend the past few weeks, talks more about Christine as he gets drunker, and gets drunker the more he talks about Christine. By 4-1, he's worried he'll lose Peter, but Peter keeps listening and ordering beer, chiming in with the odd "Good riddance" or "You're better off."

It's 5-1 when the horn goes to end the second period. Peter asks for the bill and insists on paying it. Outside the bar in a light rain, they bro-hug and get into separate cabs, Peter heading to East York while Hugh rides northwest and tries to tune out the argument in Spanish the driver's having in his earpiece. Its intensity picks up but Hugh's trying to focus on what a positive night he's had. It felt good to open up to Peter—and, it turns out, there's a chance with Kelly. As the cab crosses Davenport he swells with confidence. Why go home? If he's fouled the nest, the damage is done, and on top of that the cabbie's into a screaming match now that Hugh thinks could only be marital.

"Can I get out here, actually?" he asks as they approach St. Clair. The eyes are hot in the rear-view but once through the intersection the car halts, blocking the bus stop while Hugh pays and gets out. The cab peels away and he stands there a moment as the rain falls harder.

This was stupid, he thinks. He's had more than enough to drink, and it's Monday. Staying out too late tonight will screw his whole week. That confident part of him still says to do it, but louder now is the sadder part underneath—the one that knows he won't sleep tonight anyway. He crosses Bathurst then waits out the red light while the westbound streetcar clacks and dings and reveals the Syc behind it, the only storefront with its lights still on. Nearly slipping on the wet rails as he crosses St. Clair next, it doesn't occur to him that showing up mostly loaded might influence Kelly's opinion of him. He pulls open the door and scans the nearly empty room; the same shaved-head guy as Saturday tends bar, with two fifty-something flies on stools in front of him, and two young women, maybe students, at the front table near the window.

Hugh sits at the opposite end of the counter from the men and doesn't interrupt their conversation about the draft next year, some kid who could save the Leafs' souls. The bartender saunters over and Hugh orders a Fifty. On the screen above, blue jerseys buzz around the offensive zone. It's 5-3. Maybe the Leafs aren't out of it yet. Maybe Hugh isn't either. On his phone, he rereads the exchange with Kelly. He types in *Sounds good* and presses Send before he can change his mind. A little nervousness creeps in, but he does his best to ignore it. This is as close to playing it cool as he gets.

He uses Facebook to look in on old friends getting married, buying houses, having babies. Refreshes Twitter until his phone's nearly dead. Two tables enter, eat and leave while he sits there. His glass empties twice. The regulars go home. The Leafs have lost long ago and now the Edmonton game is on. A couple walks in, looks the place over, then turns right back out the door, which is fair. When I was there it reminded me of the bars we went to in high school, places rough around the edges where they didn't read your ID closely—especially if you looked like the two women still at the front table. The one with her back to the window has a blonde pixie-cut and wears a drapey green sweater. Hugh can see her face, and though the lighting's bad he's sure he's never seen her before—she's not Kelly with new hair. As for her friend, though, he can see only her back: a tight, white, cashmere sweater and long, dark hair. For all he knows, she's the woman I saw Sunday morning, who might have snuck into his apartment—

No, he thinks, catching himself staring. *For starters, she seems to actually exist.*

He looks into his glass then at the women again. Their conversation seemed serious earlier but they've been laughing more loudly and frequently the last little while. The one has to be the woman from outside his building or Hugh has to be sure she isn't. Sending over drinks to start a conversation is seeming like a better and better idea. *So why not?*

Because you'll seem like a creep, says the same part of Hugh that knew earlier he should go home. He doesn't actually expect to get anywhere, but on the other hand he's never tried this or any other bar pick-up move. He was barely drinking age when he met Christine, and wouldn't call the way they got together picking her up. The dorm was a false economy where everyone had just one thing in common, the fear of suddenly being an adult—or did that only apply to the two of them? In the beginning they were drunk every time they were together, home from the same bar or, if different ones, sitting at their computers checking if the other was really "Busy" like their instant messenger status said. They eventually limped into official couple status, not starting a night sober until they had been sleeping together for more than a year, and until moving to Toronto, one or the other or sometimes both at once would pass into periods of hurt or anger or worst, general indifference, occasionally for weeks at a time. He'd call it on-and-off, if that weren't too jovial for what they actually were.

She finally saw through you, the voice says now.

The server says, "Last call," Monday's an early close. Hugh orders one more.

It hurts to recall the Off switches, and this is far from the first time he's gotten drunk and stewed over them. He stood Christine up at a friend's party, completely blasted one Saturday night when I came to his student-house to visit. (That's why I never met her.) Another time, he made a louder-than-he-thought joke about a three-way with her cousin Judy—that time being Judy's wedding day, minutes after he was introduced to her. He got thrown out of the bar at Christine's father's sixtieth birthday, too—at four in the afternoon—and not six months ago, Christine locked herself in the bathroom and prayed he would calm down after she told him he needed to drink less.

This is what you do, the voice says. *You get something going right then trip your self-destruct, again and again, and never think of who you take out with you.*

You put Christine through hell for years.

She said, though, that she forgave him—six months ago when he'd smashed the wall, and again last month when she ended things for good. She said not to forget that, either: they were fine on paper (whatever that meant), but things had gotten away from them (another cliché).

She let you off the hook, the voice says, and it's true. In her words, she'd set him free—free to stop playing along and go find what he really wanted.

His beer arrives and he says, "Offer those girls a last round on me."

The bald man's eyebrows rise.

"I don't think so."

"Are you cutting me off?"

"It's last call. You should pay your tab and go home."

"I'll ask them myself, then," Hugh says.

The barkeep grabs Hugh's arm with a strong one of his own and holds tightly. It's painful. "I won't charge you for the last one," he says, his eyes drilling into Hugh's. "But you have to go. *Now.*"

Hugh lowers his head and mutters, "All right." He stands up and from his wallet produces two twenties, which he lays on the bar. He turns to leave but stops to pull out a third bill. "For the last one, and the round for the girls."

The bartender shakes his head and says, "I cover my own staff." Hugh feels the women watching as he puts the money away and heat climbs from his chest to his throat. He looks again and confirms. The blonde isn't Kelly. The dark one's unfamiliar. He's unsure how much they heard, but it doesn't matter—the bartender will fill them in, and he or they will warn Kelly against going out with him, and if Hugh ever comes here again, he'll be tossed right back into St. Clair Avenue.

There's nothing to do but go.

Outside, it's pouring now, and though he has the shoulder bag he took to work, his umbrella isn't in there, it's still packed in a box somewhere.

He begins the walk home thinking, *I can't even look good on paper anymore.*

*

He drops his soaked button-up and slacks over the bedroom radiator and changes into pyjama pants and a T-shirt. In the kitchen, he rinses the Freddy Krueger glass and fills it, chugs the water and fills again. He'll need a few more yet. Peter can't admit to a hangover tomorrow, so neither can Hugh. He drinks again, fills again, and takes the glass to the living room, where ten half-full boxes and a few bags line the walls, surrounded by things he strewed around while he searched for other things. He'd left the shared house suddenly, sorting nothing, just jamming it into boxes. In this state the apartment feels much smaller. He picks up a remote control from the coffee table and remembers me saying to unpack the TV last. If he had, at least a few boxes would be broken down in the recycling bins by now— *But then, what would I do while I tried to sober up for work?*

With the remote he brings up the streaming service and when the loading bar clears, his menu has jumped to the newly added titles, which is weird; normally, it defaults to what he watched last. He shrugs. It's just as well that new choices are available—he's not in the mood for one more episode of one more sitcom about couples or friends who'll be together forever or another needlessly violent movie that's now turning into a series, more fantastical comic books made into too-real war stories. When did escapism stop letting you escape? What about the wacky old stuff like—

Yeah, like *The X-Files*. Dead centre under *Just Added*. Excellent. When we were teenagers, we'd fill our faces with chips in front of it every Sunday night, the weekend's last flight from reality before going back to school in the morning. It's the only weird thing I ever knew Hugh to watch. He'd be grumpy by the end when an episode didn't feature the Smoking Man or advance the government cover-up plot, but myself, I loved them all, even the monsters-of-the-week meant just to freak you out—like the one highlighted on the menu he's trying to browse away from. None of the arrow buttons move the selector so he presses Enter, Menu, even Power, hoping something will happen; when nothing does, he flips the remote to open the battery compartment.

The lamp beside the couch browns.

A high-pitched buzz descends on the apartment.

The picture on the screen shakes then turns black.

The light goes out entirely.

Ah, the power just—

The lamp comes back on, intensely bright. Hugh squints and reaches under the shade for the switch but pulls his hand back: it's *hot*. He bends down instead to unplug the cord, but before he can the bulb gives out with a *snap* and the room is dark again. Startled, on hands and knees on the floor, he listens for any sound but the buzz. Light from the TV faintly returns; the black screen displays an episode number, a title and a loading meter that crawls to full. He breathes in and finally unplugs the lamp then rises to his feet, wondering if there's been a power surge. For all the times he's heard the term, he doesn't actually know anything about them—

He's knocked back onto the couch, shoulders pinned to the cushions behind him.

The episode starts.

He can't move. He can't even blink.

*

He had forgotten about Skinner, the assistant FBI director, who had just enough power to protect Mulder and Scully's work but nowhere near what was needed to expose the secrets the Smoking Man kept hinting at. He'd forgotten this episode, too, which begins with Skinner hesitating to sign his divorce papers, then going to a hotel bar, meeting an aggressive blonde and getting a room where she rolls on top of him. Just when Skinner's about to come, she turns into an enormous, screaming crone.

Cut to Skinner waking later, and the blonde's dead beside him with her neck broken.

The opening theme rolls.

Hugh's paralyzed, but inside feels like he's shaking. The woman's here with him, he's sure of it, humming the bass notes under the *do-do-do-do, do-do-do-do-do* and whistling along to the interludes. He thinks of trying to move an arm but doesn't see the point. The high-pitched buzz hasn't stopped. Mulder and Scully discover the blonde was a prostitute, and in the street outside the police station, Skinner, who has no memory of the night before, sees the crone again in a red raincoat with the hood up—but when he catches up to her, Mulder and Scully on his heels, she turns out to be Skinner's wife, who's heard what happened (and apparently, owns a similar coat). Scully next learns that Skinner's been treated for REM Sleep Behaviour Disorder, which might explain how he could kill the prostitute without remembering: in his dream, he was fighting the old woman, who would suffocate him if he didn't get her off his chest.

Mulder, as always, has a different theory: Skinner's been visited by a succubus, an entity that visits men in their dreams and can become so attached that she'll kill a romantic rival. It doesn't seem like the right explanation, and as Skinner struggles to save his career and marriage and the head of the escort agency turns up dead, we learn he's being set up—he's one more layer between the government and Mulder and Scully's work, so he's a target. (Smoking Man *is* in this one!) Skinner shows up in the bordello near the end, just in time to intercept the assassin who's about to kill a third escort—sorry, I shouldn't spoil it—and after that, when he's back at his desk and murder allegations no longer hang over him, he won't tell who tipped him off.

He says just before the credits roll that whatever he thinks happened, it has no place in an official report.

No one would believe a story about someone haunting dreams.

The even spookier end theme plays the episode out and Hugh hopes hearing it means he can get up.

He tries wriggling free of the couch. His shoulders separate a bit from the cushion—

And let go entirely—

His forehead smashes into the coffee table—

And his back's again pinned to the couch. The pale face swamped with black hair bears down, licking red lips. Hips press hard into his. The long fingernails dig into his chest and cut off his air. She's going to kill him this time. The buzz is a deafening squeal. He pushes all his willpower into twisting his shoulders away, to bucking her off before she can take him in, but his straining mind is powerless over his muscles. He can't fight it. He aches everywhere and the tissue in his penis burns. His heart pounds harder as the woman rides faster, breasts bouncing, nipples hidden by black hair he wants to push aside, he wants to feel them, wants to—

His whole body shudders. The woman collapses into him, then her weight dissipates. He listens to the apartment as he catches his breath. The electrical buzz is finally gone and the only sound is the fridge belt, *Oh my little pretty one*—

The pipe in the wall interrupts, the whoosh of water from a flushed toilet that could be anywhere in the building. Only a couple of minutes have passed. He didn't hear a door or windows, but she could already be back to her apartment—

"Stop," he says to himself, his mouth proving he can move again. These thoughts are ridiculous. He was awake the whole time.

He reaches for the water glass that's still half full and his right arm responds. He exhales, drinks, then walks to the kitchen for more. His mind's sober now but his equilibrium is still off and he teeters. He puts an arm out to catch himself on the opposite wall and his hand finds the paint-spattered doorknob that doesn't twist. His eyes move to the frame, where the paint's still unbroken. *She didn't leave through here*, he thinks—

didn't leave at all, slinkily dismount, walk a fine, bare ass away or really, even come in.

His jaw sinks into a frown regardless and he admits it to himself: couch or bed, home or not, he can't do anything to stop her. The last forty-eight hours have caught up to him and his eyes are closing as he walks to the bathroom to clean himself. In *Ghostbusters,* Venkman at least had his pants taken off first.

Beside the tub, Hugh strips, turns on the shower and sits in the tub, where he curls his body around the detachable head and hugs the hot water close.

His face creases everywhere it can. With a soft wail, he begins to weep.

TUESDAY

HE'S IN BED ATOP THE BLANKETS, freezing. In the night, he awoke in the bathtub with his extremities wrinkled like prunes and the shower, cold, still running. He half-way dried himself, unsure how long he'd slept, then staggered to bed where he lay until now, when his alarm sounds. There's plenty of time to get to work; he can even be early and make up for yesterday. He just has to get up.

If he *can* get up—

He isn't pinned, though, just lethargic, and when he does move, he rolls toward his phone and presses Snooze; maybe asleep, maybe awake, he presses it four more times, once every ten minutes, and now he's running late. His limbs are weak. The alarm sounds again and he holds his phone after silencing it. Peter will never let him live it down—being on-time after the Leafs game no matter how hungover you are is an unwritten rule, a badge of honour—but after a moment Hugh taps the office number in his contacts and leaves a voicemail saying he's sick.

He lies back then and closes his eyes, feeling as though he could sleep all day and probably needing to, but an uneasiness creeps from his lower back into his chest and shoulders, his throat, then snaps his eyes back open. He springs to a sitting position, turns and puts his feet on the floor. He can't risk staying on his back any longer. Standing to pull on clean grey boxers and a green T-shirt, he avoids his reflection in the mirror we propped against the wall Saturday. He can't handle seeing a wound on his chest again, still doesn't think he really did, and doesn't want to see a welt from the coffee table on his forehead where it hurts. And more than these, it's his eyes he won't face. He doesn't want to know what *scared to go to sleep* looks like.

In the kitchen, he slides a spoon under the flap of a new box of rice cereal and dumps some into one of the three mismatched bowls Christine spent years asking him to get out of the basement. He still hears her voice: *You'll need them again, is that it? Are you planning to leave me or something?* Her list of deal-breakers was always growing, but something he hasn't thought about until now is the increasing frequency with which she insinuated he wanted to go. Had he sent that message? He doesn't know that he sent any message at all. Maybe that was the problem. Maybe it wouldn't have been hard to make her feel more secure.

He cracks the seal on the milk carton, tips it into the bowl, and when he turns to replace it in the fridge, he pauses. *The locked door.* He studies the knob a moment before remembering yesterday's slacks, draped over the bedroom rad. If one of the keys in the pockets fits… He retrieves them, but none of the three labelled with bits of masking tape *#10*, *Ext Door* or even the longshot *Mail #10* works. He drops them on the counter and takes up the bowl and spoon, drowning out the fridge's bleating as he chews only to hear it anew when he swallows. A bit queasy from the milk meeting last night's beer, he leaves the kitchen to find his phone.

Nick sounds like he's eating as well when he picks up, and in the background Hugh hears at least two children protesting against going to school.

"Oh yeah, shoulda told ya." Hugh hears him swallow. "Superintendent in the seventies wanted a bigger suite for himself, so lucky you, Number Eight's bedroom became your kitchen and now that unit's a bachelor. They never changed it back when they stopped using on-site supers."

"So the door?"

"Was the bedroom door. I guess it was cheaper to put on a lock than fill in the doorway—it's keyed on both sides, you don't need to worry."

"Who has the key?"

"Just me," Nick says. "The neighbour can't get into your place or anything."

"Is the neighbour away, by the way? There's a lot of mail piled up under the door."

"Oh, shit, I should've mentioned that, too: it's up for repairs this month, no one's there. The last tenant trashed it pretty bad. We have to drywall again." Nick pauses, maybe thinking. "We could just cover the door on that side. Would that make you feel better?"

"Yeah, it could," Hugh says.

"Another thing I should have mentioned: if you get someone else's mail in your box, just take it to their door and slide it under, okay? The other tenants will do the same for you. It's not a policy or anything, it's just nice."

Hugh says, "Okay." It really sounds like a policy. "What did you mean, trashed?"

"Trashed."

"Like, something horrible?"

"The holes in the walls, the cockroaches, the cat piss smell that'll never leave… yeah, I'd say it's horrible." Through the phone Hugh hears a door shut and then no more kids' voices. Nick breathes out heavily. "Why? What do *you* mean?"

"I don't know." Hugh stays silent for a moment. *Ghosts don't exist,* he tells himself. *Ghosts, demons, none of the crap in* X-Files *or the movies Bobby watches.* But he has no other explanation. A ghost is less out-there than—what was it called, a *succubus*? His mouth goes dry.

"Like, nobody was murdered there or anything, right?"

Nick laughs. "Oh, wow. No. Ha!" He eases into a quiet chuckle. "For all the rentals I've done, no one's ever asked me that, you know." He seems to think for a second. "I've been managing buildings sixteen years... knock on wood, I've never had a tenant die in their unit."

Hugh taps the door frame with his knuckles then thanks Nick and disconnects. The cereal has gone mushy but he takes it to the coffee table anyway. He knows the switch on the lamp can't still be hot, but he pinches it cautiously. It's room-temperature. The light doesn't come on and he lets out a relieved breath. Something that seemed to happen last night *did* happen: the bulb burned out.

He picks up the remote control next. The streaming service loads normally with his recently watched list back at the top. *X-Files* is nowhere in sight and the sitcom is ready to go. The show's vapid, but it got him through the weeks at Peter's house, three or four episodes at a time while he was trying not to think, *What do I do now?* or *Where did I go wrong with her?* He presses Play and the episode starts, which shouldn't surprise him, but after last night, does. He chews the slushy cereal and laughs half-heartedly at the show's first joke.

Now he's trying to not think about being Nick's first.

*

On the wooden pass above the ravine his slapping shoes resonate over crashing power chords, the one-two bass and snare to which Bon snarls he wants no conversation, just sweet sensation—*to make a meal out of you 'cause I'm a love (love!) hun-gry man*. It's as dirty as *My Sharona* and, though Hugh hasn't considered it before, predatory somehow doesn't seem like the right approach for Bon, who just three songs ago, while out on the town and looking for a woman, was shot down in flames.

His feet move from wood to pavement. He's endured the run, and survived the stairs, and feels he can get up the small hill that connects the bridge to the boulevard, like he might even get home without breaking stride, but slows to a walk. He called in sick, but he's not sick, he just needs sleep—and now that he's cleared his head and tired himself out, there's no need to flatline, not even if he's tempted to reproduce yesterday's conditions and see if he'll be attacked again. He still doesn't remember getting home, stripping off his sweaty clothes or getting into bed, nothing.

Beside the grassy island, his breathing calms. Last night's rain rises as vapour from a hedge sunlit in the cool air. Three minutes later, he's climbing his building's steps. He checks his mailbox and finds nothing, which disappoints him but shouldn't. He hasn't shared his new address with anyone but me, not even Human Resources, and decides he shouldn't delay: he bought three months of forwarding, and when it expires he doesn't want Christine texting to ask where he lives so she can drop off mail that came to the house, which she would do because it would make her feel better about some aspect of the end of their relationship and that would clearly be more important than however he might feel about seeing her again. She'll save the mail even if Chase has already moved in, which Hugh is pretty sure he has, and she won't even hide it—as she gathers it up, Chase will say something about him and they'll laugh together. Hugh tells himself he doesn't care, that he doesn't have to anymore and doesn't want to see her again ever, under any circumstance—and as for Chase, he thinks, *He might not totally kick my ass,* humouring himself as he arrives at his door. *I can't be so out of shape: I mean, Kelly wants some—*

> *Though her boss could kick my ass—*
> *The pixie-cut server will point me out—*
> *Or the dark-haired one—*

He leaves his key in his lock and turns back toward Apartment Eight, where he squats to examine the pile of letters. Only after he's touched an envelope does he stop himself. Stealing mail is illegal. Standing again, he surveys the ceiling to either end of the hall. When he sees no cameras, he exhales, but with the relief comes disappointment: he didn't imagine until right now that security footage could catch someone coming or going from his apartment, and now that he has the idea is of no use anyway.

He won't keep the letters, he just needs to see. He pulls one out by its corner and reads the name.

Elise Pappadopoulous.

It sounds dark-haired.

He slides it back under the door and returns to his own. At his coffee table, he hunches over his laptop and googles her: she's a hair stylist in Chicago, or a Montreal high school valedictorian in the nineties, or the allegedly Los Angeles-based owner of a Facebook profile in which Hugh can't be sure she's the same woman from photo to photo. He tries again—"Elise Pappadopoulos Toronto"—and gets a hit on LinkedIn: a student at York. A different Facebook profile shows the same woman in a mortarboard and a black gown with a red hood. She chose the spring convocation.

It's just a theory, but to Hugh, it feels like a good one. Didn't he get his own unit at a moment's notice and a low price, like a student might? And wouldn't only irresponsible young people trash an apartment? (No offense, Elise.)

He laughs a little. He doesn't actually know her. She looks as Greek as she sounds, though, with a Mediterranean complexion and curls in her dark hair, unlike the woman he's been seeing, who's pale with hair as straight as the woman in *The Ring*, which we saw when we were teenagers. (It's not as scary as the original from Japan, but it still freaked the hell out of Hugh, the idea that something could stalk you through a screen…)

He clicks the red X to close all seven tabs of Elises and lets his eyes drift to the actual window. The blinds are closed so he stands up and opens them, letting in what little light isn't blocked by the building beside his. He stares at the bricks for a long moment then admits it might be time to talk to someone— someone different this time, though, not the guy who's been counselling Christine's family for years, who Hugh accepted to see when he could no longer get through a month, a week, a day without making one more irrevocable remark, one more irreparable mistake. He never stopped Hugh from thinking everything was his fault, never probed deeper to see if maybe he was the unsatisfied one or maybe Christine was as wrong for him as he was for her. How did Hugh ever think seeing him was a good idea? He wants to never remember it again, not this nor any other decision they made together ostensibly to help him but really to turn him into who she wanted him to be—someone he never was, someone he isn't.

Around the apartment are scattered piles and boxes of who he is, who he still is or at least, what's left of him.

He sets to work unpacking them.

*

With the boxes broken down and piled by the door to take to the recycling bin, he opens a tote bag of papers shoved in hastily from the large desk he and Christine shared. He folds the ones that are hers into an envelope he'll stamp and mail tomorrow. But should it be this easy? He's suspicious of his impassivity, this feeling no more affecting than expelling the last phlegm from a long cold. Among some shirts he gathers to hang are two Christine gave him; on the windowsill, a plant she bequeathed and he's watered just enough to not kill. In the bathroom, some cologne is from her, scents he's never worn save for a couple of formal nights when she put on one of the two dresses he loved, the blue one or his favourite, purple with tiny straps and hemmed on an angle, revealing one thigh and making it impossible to think of anything but the other.

The physical reminders will go in time, but the mental ones will stay. He has yet to shower after his run and still thinks of the purple dress, of peeling it off her after dinner in Acapulco one discount winter weekend six years ago. He removes his clothes in the bathroom with his memory playing its Best of Christine reel and, as though unconsciously, his left hand clutches his cock while he opens the water with the other and his mind calls up the black negligee after his last college exam, the eyes hazy from the half-drunk wine bottle on the night table. He steps into the shower seeing the faces she made, how big her eyes got when she—

Long, dark hair—bared teeth, sharp and shining. He braces himself on the shower tile before she takes his breath and leaves his mouth hanging open.

His shoulders buckle, his hips surge.

He stands trembling after, the hand on the wall supporting him and water running down his back until he finally begins to wash. The woman's in his brain. She's eating his memories.

He turns the water off and wraps himself in a towel. The faucet drips to a silence that freezes him staring at the ceramic floor, its black and white tiles becoming starker as the steam clears. He knows he can move, but can't convince himself to lift a leg out of the tub. He's not just tired, he's ashamed. His lecherous mind has completely unmoored from reality. But then, he dries a foot and wills it onto the cold floor. What else is he supposed to do? The second follows and they lead him to the wood floor in the hallway.

Naked but for the towel and having forgotten to close the blinds, he hurries past the living room window without looking down—without watching for nails. Below his instep, his flesh tears. His mouth grunts a *Fuck!* Blood shoots from the long cut and he drops to one knee, pressing the towel to his foot then scuffling back to the bathroom where he sits on the toilet lid and wads paper to stop the bleeding. Does he need stitches? How does he get to the hospital—should he call an ambulance? He's never been injured badly while alone—he's never been injured badly in general. He takes more paper and soaks it in cold water so it won't stick. The blood begins to clot. On the floor the sight of the piled-up, red-blotched mound makes him light-headed.

He lists and falls.

Water, he thinks—*they give people water after they donate blood*—but he's on his back now and unable to move, unable to look away from the black mould in the flaking ceiling paint. A tapping sound is approaching like footsteps, intensifying until his ears ring. *Black mould.* The woman descends on him, heavier than ever. He's not ready to go again. *Black mould, black mould…*

How do I make her stop?

The name from next door is suddenly on his tongue and he pleads to breathe the E, to push the L off his alveolar ridge, a blind stab with no idea what will happen if he succeeds. Will she disintegrate? Will she finally look him in the eye? His chest feels like it's being crushed, his sternum about to shatter, the cry of the orgasm he doesn't want is in his throat, *blackmouldblackmouldblackmouldblack—*

"Elise!"

She's already gone when he says it, though, and he's again alone on his back with a sad white puddle on his belly. He breathes in through his nose and smells the musty ceiling for the first time. Closing his eyes, he lets the mould grow over him, the black the only thing he can see.

*

When I commuted, I'd wake up around four-thirty, get on the QEW a little after that then follow the Gardiner and Eastern to whichever soundstage we were on. I could usually get out without waking Cole, and sometimes Kate wouldn't stir, either, but for the last month she'd been too pregnant to sleep much and was getting up with me and making a pot of coffee out of habit, putting twenty ounces in my travel mug then dumping the rest as she couldn't drink it just then.

The highway was quiet this morning; it usually was, though some days in the left lane someone would materialize in my mirror from nowhere, going to beat hell for a reason I could only guess at. Alone again once they'd flown by, I'd get caught up imagining what they were running from, how long they'd been running now, and I'd get to work pretty thankful to have not had an accident, remembering nothing from the drive but having made up a story the way I've been making up Hugh's since I last talked to him.

Around the Hurontario exit, my phone vibrated in my pocket, and though I knew I shouldn't look, it could've been Kate. The baby could've been coming. I didn't have a hands-free kit, and still don't—it'll be built into my next truck if I ever get around to getting one. I glanced up and down, road to phone, and read the message even though it wasn't her.

It was from Hugh, a huge string of texts.

The ghost woman you saw won't let me sleep
It's been three straight nights
Sometimes twice or three times a night
She even got me while I was outside once
I'm on my bathroom floor
I don't think I'm going to live

—A long horn blasted from my right and I hit the brakes as a cube van crossed into my lane, its tail nearly catching my front corner before I swerved toward the meridian I'd have hit if I didn't wrench the wheel back in time, dropping the phone to the floor where I couldn't retrieve it until I got to work, which was just as well. It was a close call. I breathed in and out deeply once, backed my speed off to about one-oh-five and triple-checked my blind spot before changing into the centre lane. I could slow down a little—hell, I could be late. Nothing was more important than meeting my little girl in a few days, or hours, or whenever it would happen. A warm feeling climbed from my chest and my mouth relaxed into a lazy smile.

Looking back, it seems clearer Hugh needed help, but I don't know, maybe I was just distracted. You don't always see what's going on while it's happening.

WEDNESDAY

MORNING LIGHT FROM THE SMALL frosted window mixes with yellow from the bulb overhead as Hugh rubs his eyes. Did he really sleep on the bathroom floor? Just one night after passing out in the shower? Did he sleep here *all night*? How long was that, twelve hours? Fourteen?

A fuzzy memory returns of frantically typing on his phone, sometime between the black mould and now, leaving off only after asking which movie it was from (yes, there were even more messages, I found them when I got to work). The *it* he was asking about was the idea that the ghost goes away if you say its name. If only. It's in so many, though it's not for ghosts, it's for demons and the way it works is, you gain control of them if you say their archaic, *true* names—which, sorry Hugh, are usually tougher to say than Pappadopoulos.

On his foot, bits of paper in the dried blood have crusted the wound in maroon. He stands on it cautiously then turns on the shower, feels the cut sting as he steps into water to wash it and the white residue on his abdomen, too. He puts peroxide on a cotton swab after and grits his teeth as the cleaner makes him dizzy, trying to recall when he last had a tetanus shot and avoid thinking of the woman, which works as well as saying, "Don't think about an elephant"—can you think of anything but? Breathing through his nose, holding his balance, he watches the white bubbles under the skin. The elephant's not in the room right now. He sticks on a bandage, wraps his towel around himself and retrieves his phone from the floor; he doesn't look at it until he reaches the bedroom, eyes scouring the hardwood for nailheads the whole way, then sets a reminder, *Canadian Tire*, for 4:55pm.

Currently, it's 7:30. He pulls on grey slacks and black socks and carries a white-and-blue checked shirt to the bathroom. In the mirror, his face is puffy, his eyes bloodshot. Patchy stubble crawls down his neck. It doesn't matter that he slept a whole night, the equivalent of two nights for a lot of people: when you're deprived, getting any just makes you want more. He runs his electric razor and brushes his teeth, then puts the shirt on, tucks it in and cinches his belt. He's surprised to look nearly presentable and still be on pace to get to work forty-five minutes early.

A few ticks past nine, though, Peter calls him crisply and any goodwill Hugh might have earned back dissipates. He rises and, dress shoe pressing against the cut on his foot, gingerly follows his boss.

With his office door closed, Peter says, "Are you still hungover?"

Hugh's shoulders tighten. *How do I put this…?*

"I'm just not sleeping right."

"That may be." Peter lowers his voice. "But everyone knows we drink on game nights. It looks really bad if you call in sick the next day."

Is he really going to give me shit? His chest constricts. *I didn't drink any more than he did.*

"I'm sorry," he manages to say.

Peter exhales and his face softens. "It's not a huge deal." He looks at Hugh's feet. "Were you limping, by the way?"

"Yeah," Hugh says. "These nails in my floorboards jump up at me once in a while." He doesn't let himself ramble this time, just tries to smile like he's shrugging it off—*you know, stupid clumsy Hugh*—but he doesn't feel convincing and Peter doesn't seem convinced.

"Are you sure you don't need more time off? You've kind of been through the wringer."

The fake smile crumbles. His breathing speeds up.

Can you trust him?

It doesn't feel like his own question—it's like someone planted it in his brain, the way someone took over his memories. He knows he should, that Peter wants them to be close—and as I haven't answered his texts, there's really no one else.

Will she let me tell him?

He makes himself breathe in deeply.

"I'm seeing a woman—"

"Kelly the waitress! Awesome."

Hugh puts a hand to his face and says, "No, I mean there's a woman… in my apartment—like, a ghost or something." There was that word again. It didn't quite fit, but was easier to say to another person than whatever Mulder might call her. "She doesn't let me sleep, and when she does, I wake up feeling worse than before."

"Yeah, take the rest of the week."

Hugh says, "Honestly, it's better to work," but he can't hide the shudder in his spine. "I don't like spending so much time alone."

Peter stands, leans over the desk and puts his hands on Hugh's shoulders. He looks squarely in his eyes. "The only ghost you're living with," he says, "is named Christine."

Hugh starts to protest but Peter's not done.

"You have till Monday to exorcise her. See a psychiatrist, a priest, a prostitute, whatever you need to do—there's no judgment and the health plan should cover it. Well, not the prostitute. And go to the doctor, too. You're probably due."

"I'm fine," Hugh says. At the doctor's office, he squirms over things way more normal than this.

"You'll be better next week. I need you focused when you're here." Peter smiles. "Go home and find some tedious, little, pain-in-the-ass task, then do it till it's done. That helps me when I start to go crazy."

"All right," Hugh says. Peter's just called him crazy but there's no point in arguing. "If it doesn't get better, though, I don't know, I might have to move again, and I might ask to stay—"

"It won't come to that." Peter looks up. Someone's gesturing at him through the glass door. "I've got a meeting. See you Monday, okay?"

Hugh nods and softly says, "Okay," feeling the irritation of Joanne in Accounts Receivable as he edges past her. Gathering his shoulder bag from the hook on his cubicle partition, he thinks of packing his personal items. It'd be impulsive to quit, there's no real reason to, but beyond a need for money there's no reason to stay, either. *Maybe Christine was right*, he thinks. Maybe he's been coasting. Maybe he should keep reading that book. He shakes his head as he bends over his computer to set his out-of-office message. He's not an entrepreneur, he doesn't have any ideas. The elevator takes him to the ground floor and he leaves the building, which is a couple of blocks from the Eaton Centre and the Canadian Tire attached to it. Ahead of him, a streetcar slows to a stop. If he runs, he'll catch it, but he doesn't and it's not because of his injured foot—it's because, for once, he has all day.

*

Bobby would be proud, he thinks as he removes his purchases from three bulging plastic bags, and he's right, I would be. He owns nail-sets now, a four-pack—a nail-set set—as well as a kit of screwdrivers, a marked-down hacksaw with changeable blades for wood, metal or fibreglass and a power drill he's not sure he needs, but it was on sale. And though unlikely to need the set of sanding and cutting bits, he bought that, too. Letting Christine call Chase for all the handyman jobs was a mistake, which I could've told Hugh, and I don't only mean because she cheated with the handyman. Anyone can learn to fix anything from videos on the internet. He'll never get as good at it as me, but as he opens the nail-set package he at least considers the possibility he's not just anyone.

     The glow wears off when he discovers how many nails are in a floor—or in this case, not-so in—and that several sizes have been used. He crawls and brushes the wood with his hand, putting his ear down from time to time to spot heads poking above the uneven surface then gathering up his hammer and, it seems, a different-coloured tool every time. The blue is smaller than the red, but bigger than the green and the yellow. The colours remind him of baby toys.

They'd almost never talked about children. Christine showed some restraint, never browbeating him specifically about how unprepared or unsuited he was to fatherhood, but she hadn't encouraged him, either—hadn't indicated either way whether she wanted him to get ready. A vicious thought brings a vengeful "Ha!": *What if Chase knocked her up?* He taps in another nail and the bile subsides. *Maybe all she wants is a good father for her kids.* In her parents' eyes, coming back from college coupled was the bigger prize than the diploma, and since bringing Hugh home, she'd mostly managed their disappointment instead of celebrating the next milestones, the wedding, the house, the baby.

It crashes in on him: he'd have been an awful father.

He's spent his whole afternoon on the nails, and the three in the corner behind the modem must be the last; it's after five and in the sparse light from the window, it appears he's driven down every one. He turns on the overhead light and finds another twenty to sink, but when it doesn't frustrate him he realizes: this is what

Peter was talking about. The power of tedium—where was *that* inspirational book?

He replaces the bulb in the living room lamp with one also bought this afternoon then removes six new tumblers from their box and washes them, resting them in the rack beside the *Nightmare* glass. The oven preheats as he stores another purchase, a cheap set of salt and pepper shakers, in the cupboard with his motley liquor collection. He pauses a moment on the bottles, an Irish whiskey at the front of them. He rarely goes for the hard stuff, but hasn't bought beer since the weekend, and now he remembers Chase brusquely handing him this bottle at his thirtieth birthday party. He barely acknowledged Hugh before beelining to Christine and wrapping her in an enormous hug that made her squeal.

When she told Hugh they were fucking, did she say for how long? How did they even meet? It's probably longer than he'd guess, and it doesn't matter now. He dries one of the new glasses, pours and raises a drink, and says, "A toast, fucker," before he takes a sip. He unwraps a pizza from the freezer. It'll take twenty minutes in the oven; he'll watch most of an episode, then another while he eats.

Entering the living room, he steps on a nailhead. *Missed one.*

The hammer and nail-sets are still on the coffee table. Hugh exchanges his glass for them, turns back and kneels. He runs his hand over what he thinks is the spot then lies down on his side and eyes the floor.

Nothing's sticking up.

He puts the hammer back and sits on the couch. The TV works, the streaming works, the new bulb in the lamp works. He sips the whiskey he sort of doesn't like and watches three quarters of the sitcom he sort of does until the oven rings. He pauses the show and rises from the couch.

His sock snags again.

He doesn't lift his foot this time, he just leans over the table and picks up the hammer. He marks the nail's position in his mind as he bends down and disentangles the thread; as he steps off, he moves his finger to where his foot was. He flattens his palm and slides it on the floor.

He feels again and again. It poked his foot—he saw it in his sock—but there's no nailhead, no sliver from a floorboard, nothing.

Scrunching his nose, scowling, he inhales. That's when he smells the smoky oven. He smacks the floor once with the hammer and unthinkingly takes it to rescue his dinner, leaving it on the counter before he opens the oven and nudges the pizza onto a plate, the crust hot on his fingertips. He closes the door, plate in one hand and knife to cut the pizza in the other, and when he finally turns toward the living room another nailhead tears his sock and bites into his foot. The plate clatters on the floor, the pizza somehow still on it and face up as he drops to his knees, yells, and smashes the hardwood with his fist—without finding another nail, for once.

When he turns back to retrieve the pizza, his eyes settle on the disused door.

She's fucking with me.

He understands now why he bought the extra tools.

The pizza will go cold on the floor. The paused sitcom will shut off automatically. Hugh brings the hacksaw down on the doorknob and pulls back and forth, scoring it without cutting much. He tears the plastic wrap off the drill's cardboard box then rips the cardboard, too. The battery needs to charge but he has to run it dead first, which I'm surprised he knows, actually. He unpacks the attachments and picks a circular one that looks to him like a blade. He squeezes the trigger. The tool whirs and applying it grows the small hacksaw cuts, making a hot, metallic smell until the battery dies, the knob only a quarter of the way off.

His heart is racing.

He detaches the battery and rams it into the charger. His breaths are short. He reclaims the hammer from the counter, lines up its head with the knob and brings it down once, again, again, smashing furiously, mangling it until he sees the lock's guts inside and wishing now he'd bought a crowbar, too. He takes his new flat-head and torques on different parts until the screwdriver's shaft breaks, then he smashes the protruding lock pieces with the hammer some more, stopping only when he's out of wind.

Has the battery charged yet? He reattaches it; it has a little juice, and he bores into the centre of the mechanism. The little clangs of pieces on the floor spur him on until he hears the knob on the other side fall. He stoops to look through the hole, but seeing only darkness, resumes battering the bolt, slamming and prying until nothing holds the door shut anymore. He sticks his hand in the hole to pull—

And his knuckles brush the back of a sheet of drywall. The yellow paint cracks inaudibly as he swings the door open and stares, the heaves in his chest subsiding. His senses return. The smell of burnt metal and lock oil mixes with smoky pizza and the oven he now knows hasn't been cleaned in years. The fridge is bleating as always, and someone is knocking at his door—pounding, actually, like they've been there a while, and yelling, "Hey! What are you doing in there!?"

The renovation, Hugh remembers. They must have heard the noise through the wall. He starts to clean up the pieces, but it's futile: however the next few minutes go, he'll get an eviction notice in the morning.

He may as well open up.

On the other side is Nick himself, in a dusty T-shirt and jeans spattered white.

"Had enough of that old door, huh?" he asks before even entering.

Hugh stands aside as Nick looks over the kitchen, where the whiskey bottle still sits on the counter.

"Can I offer you a drink?" he deadpans.

Nick snorts, almost laughing.

"Why the hell not?"

Hugh dries one of the new glasses and pours. *This could be going worse.* He hands it to Nick.

"Had to see what was on the other side, is that it?"

"Someone's been coming in through that door," Hugh says. "A woman."

"Impossible." Nick sips the whiskey. "Got any ice?" Hugh shakes his head. Nick shrugs and surveys the damage. "You could've asked to see the other unit… I mean, the mud's still drying, but I've already shown it, there's such a rental shortage. It should go this week." He eyes Hugh. "Unless they get a whiff of their crazy neighbour."

"Who's Elise Pappadopoulos?"

"Elise was eighty-six years old, had five cats and still smoked in her unit." Nick laughs. "She was a hoarder, too, a real fire hazard. Her son finally convinced her to move in with him and his wife last month. He'd been paying her rent for years."

Hugh nods, unsure what to say next but wanting to look like he's in thought.

"What's it to you?" Nick asks.

"I'm seeing things, and weird things are happening—I hammered down every nail in the floor today but they're popping back up, I swear. I've been injured. I can't sleep anymore."

"So you...?"

"So I think this place is haunted."

Nick's mouth hangs half-open as Hugh pursues him.

"Be honest with me. Did Elise die next door? Maybe she's got her young body back—or maybe it's *my* apartment, maybe one of the old superintendents?" He can't believe he hasn't considered a super yet.

Nick says, "I don't believe in ghosts." He looks past the fridge once more. "And I don't believe what you did to that door, either." He turns back to Hugh, who avoids his eyes. "I need to keep your deposit to fix it, but I can let you out of your lease at the end of the month. Feel free to go sooner."

"Okay," Hugh says.

Nick frowns. "You seemed like such a sure bet." He starts toward the apartment's main door. "Wouldn't be the first time, I guess."

"I'm sorry," Hugh says.

"Yeah, me too."

After Nick pulls the door shut, Hugh returns to the kitchen and puts the pizza in the microwave. When it's hot again, he takes it to the living room, and the bottle of whiskey, too.

*

Every episode is different, but every episode is the same: one of the couples moves forward with something they agree on, the other has some kind of disagreement, and the wacky, single friends, one male, one female, keep having wacky adventures while still seeming to have endless time to morally support the couples. Hugh's watched it play out four times in a row now, refreshing his whiskey with each new episode, and has reached the end of a season. There wasn't even a cliff-hanger. One man proposed to one woman and she accepted, so next season will be all about the wedding; if that doesn't get ratings, maybe the other couple will get unexpectedly pregnant, and if that doesn't work, the show will just be cancelled and its premise reincarnated in yet another series he'll hear is good, *finally* start watching, become increasingly disappointed with, but watch to the end anyway.

If he can't sleep anymore, though, what else should he do than catch up on series and movies everyone but him has seen? This is home and there's nowhere else—no friends who'll believe him, none who could take him in, and no way he could afford a hotel now that he needs first and last rent on a new apartment by the end of the month. He just paid first and last on this one.

And if he stayed somewhere else, what would it matter? She showed him when he was out running: she'll find him wherever he goes.

He sighs and adjusts his thought: *I'll wig out anywhere. That's all that's happening.* Visitations don't really happen—suggestible, vulnerable people just come to believe they do. A glitch in the streaming service or a stuck button on the remote chose the *X-Files* episode. That's the only thing it could have been.

He picks up his phone, hoping I answered his messages. I didn't—what do you even say when someone melts down like that?—but he thinks I'm his only hope. Aren't I into horror movies, like kind of way too into horror movies? And wasn't it me who saw the woman Sunday in front of his building? He can count on me to not tell him it's all in his head—can't he?

I don't know. I've already told you, I don't actually believe in this stuff.

Under the conversation with me is the one with Kelly.

Whenever ur free, she had said.

He looks at the bottle, at the surprisingly small dent he's made. "How else are you going to change anything?" he asks aloud. "Sit here and drink all night?"

He types a few attempts—*Working tonight?*, *What time do you get off?*, *Still up for that drink?*—and erases them all. If she's not working, she likely has plans or she's sick. Asking what time is too expectant, especially if she isn't at work. And what if she isn't still up for it?

How about tonight?

It's confident, but not cocky, and picks up the conversation where they left it—no preamble, straight to the point, which she might like. She hasn't danced around anything yet. He presses Send before he can read it over again, sure that if he does he'll spend the next hour typing and erasing and eventually write a message so long and wishy-washy he'll give up—or worse, send that.

His phone buzzes.

It's slow, let me see

Second text:

I can go at 11. Meet me here?

He thinks about the bartender—the forceful grip, the nose that's clearly been broken and probably more than once. Maybe he won't be there, though. Maybe he won't care. People get drunk in bars sometimes, right?

There's Peter's advice to consider, too. The *maybe.*

Maybe we can go somewhere else.
Idk where, she replies. *Its raining pretty hard*
Ok, Hugh writes. *11 at Syc*
Ya
See you then
K

Now he has to pick a shirt and find clean jeans. Brush off his shoes. Now he has to pack a condom in his wallet, doesn't he? He's getting ahead of himself—and hasn't bought any, anyway. He opens the cabinet in the bathroom and, seeing the cologne bottles pushed into a cluster at the back, gathers them into the small garbage can, ties the bag and sets it by the door to drop in the bin on the way out. It'll never be his thing. He locates his umbrella in the bedroom closet after a longer-than-hoped-for search and then he's ready; ten-twenty, with just a fifteen-minute walk between him and the bar. He doesn't put on music, doesn't start another sitcom episode, doesn't pick up the business book—he just sits finishing the latest glass of whiskey and thinking.

Kelly's called his bluff—my bluff, originally—and now he has to show his hand. He feels like a pair of sevens: maybe enough to win, but he won't know until he sees the final card. He's no deadbeat, Peter reminded him, but there's a limit on how much he can spit-shine his utter averageness. A stable (i.e., boring) job and an apartment of his own are low bars—what about *him* would interest someone like Kelly, who could have anyone in Toronto she wants or just as easily pick up and move indefinitely to another continent *because you know, it was just getting stale and the guys were all stupid and had baggage…*

Oh, does he. He feels the night already slow-rolling into a train wreck, feels his head spin a bit as he empties his glass and the whiskey burns his throat. Four drinks at home by himself: another great selling point.

What else did Peter say, though? *You just don't tell women anymore.* There are so many clichés, so many shameless pick-up tricks and slimy websites and scumbags banned from entering the country to give seminars while so many more scumbags scream "Free speech!" like it's their licence to be soulless. Hugh won't deceive anyone—he couldn't even laugh at Barney Stinson's playbook when he finally got around to that series—but that doesn't mean he has to lead with his worst qualities. He has to be more confident, is all. His job is average, but it's secure; the eviction sucks, but it's not false to just say he's looking for a better apartment. It's about projecting positively. Where did he hear that term—was it in the business book? If he's going to date in any serious way, he'll be evaluated against a woman's checklist for life partner and probably father of her children. He has to show a little maturity.

But is he mature? Or is he just the first non-threatening guy she's encountered in a while? *Do women do that?* he wonders. Do they set out to just get laid like a lot of men do, but select only on the basis of how unlikely the guy is to hurt them?

He can't imagine hurting a woman, especially his girlfriend or someday, wife—and yet, he came close once. He didn't touch her, didn't say he was going to hurt her, but still Christine locked herself in the bathroom, hiding and afraid. He knows he was loud, was yelling, but that's all. He wishes he could remember more, but after watching the Leafs at the bar with Peter that Friday night, there's nothing until the next day when she sat on the nice couch and asked him to take the matching armchair facing her, their usual we-need-to-talk setup. He doesn't know now what they said, and he's pretty sure *I'm sorry* featured prominently in his part—but in his morning-after bleariness, did he hear her at all? She had been *scared* of him. She shouldn't have needed to say more, but he talked in circles defending himself, explaining his actions, and never said the least of what she probably needed to hear most: that he'd never act like that again—though he would, for just for a second more, when she told him about Chase and ended things—and that he'd get help for his drinking, anger or both.

He's ashamed now of his rebuttals, of arguing as though she were crazy to think a drunk roaring at her through a locked door might hurt her. And it doesn't matter that most days he doesn't feel angry or that he hasn't been in a fight since he was a kid, or that it had never happened with her before—something brought it out, and one time was too many.

Did he come across like a ticking bomb? Had she been walking on eggshells all along, expecting it? They met at twenty-two and Hugh feels like he's stayed that age since. (It would explain the Kelly thing.) He stood still for years, parked in front of a TV and always another beer. He doesn't remember the last day he went without drinking. Meanwhile, Christine advanced, twice moving into a better job, while all Hugh earned was a five-year award that came with a hundred-dollar gift card redeemable—where else—but at the grocery chain he worked for. She swallowed her pride and got help from her parents to move into the house, too, covering the first month herself and borrowing the last because Hugh somehow never saved any money. He said he'd pay it back when he got a promotion or a decent raise but neither came.

The last few years, he saw she wasn't satisfied, but if he's honest with himself, he sees he did nothing to fix it. Like a child, he took criticism as attacks on his person and piled them higher inside himself, and in the end, the morning after cornering her in a bathroom, tried to say her disappointment with him was actually her own fault.

If it's about what you did, it's guilt—but it's shame when it's about what you are.

When she told him about Chase, he didn't punch the wall wishing it was her. He knows that. He wasn't angry with her, not for leaving, cheating or anything at all.

He was angry at himself.

And now it's time to go. He picks up his phone and considers bailing by text or just ghosting, just not showing up and never answering any messages Kelly might send wondering what happened to him, whether she would ever see him again, whether he died or was abducted or something. It feels unlikely she'd care—but what if she would? What if he can start over, on the right foot this time? They can be together a long time, or maybe not so long. Maybe it'll be a fling and end in a couple of weeks when he moves again, finds a new bar near his new place and avoids dating the staff, no matter what.

Knowing he's leaving, fouling this nest doesn't seem so bad anymore. And the alternative, just trying to go to sleep, feels more dangerous. Alone with it all, he sends me a text, ignoring that I ignored his last one. *I'm going to meet Kelly right now.* A bad feeling comes over him, as though he's bragging, but I guess he figured I'd want to know, and I did. I was watching *The Haunting* again at the time—not the shitty nineties one, the original—and Kate, super-pregnant as she was, wasn't feeling well and had gone to bed. I knew she wasn't sleeping, and I should've been with her. I should've been in bed myself given that I had to leave for work before sunrise, but nobody sleeps those last days before the due date: everything's in position, everyone's on edge, and anything that happens is either another overwhelming hint a miracle's upon you or another landmine you have no way of not stepping on and blowing into a screaming, crying fight about nothing. I should've been showing my support—not *doing* anything, just being there—but I don't know, I'm kind of a kid sometimes.

If he wanted advice about how to make a relationship work, I didn't have any, but I guess I thought I remembered something from before I met Kate, from that time before social media or eHarmony when you might just go out and meet someone—when people just talked to each other.

Ask her questions about herself, I wrote back. *Make it about her, not you.*

He reads the message and rises from the couch.

*

Inside the Syc, he closes the still-dripping umbrella. The rain came on a strong wind and his jeans are wet from the thighs down. He didn't rush, but feels out of breath.

Above the liquor wall, competing speakers blast thundering eighties hair-rock and the sound from a San Jose Sharks game no one's watching. If the bar weren't so close to his apartment, there'd be nothing to recommend it.

Kelly sits in a booth at the back, working out her tips. Hugh remembered she was pretty, but he's struck dumb in the entrance by her blonde hair, small nose, and casual black dress. She raises her head just before he can look away, holds up a *one-minute* finger and smiles. Her teeth are perfect and white, her eyes are bright.

He's way out of his league.

From the kitchen at the back, the shaved-head bartender storms toward him. Kelly stands and follows, asking, "Max?" as he barks over the music, "*Out!*" and points at the door. The black T-shirt stretched across his muscular chest makes Hugh feel lucky to have not been killed last time. He turns and spills out the door recessed from the street, sheltering there from the rain until Max brings his face to the glass and shouts, "*Go!*"

From under the next awning, Hugh peeks through the window. Max is lecturing Kelly with his back to Hugh, his index finger raised. She glances subtly toward Hugh, but not subtly enough, which makes Max wheel and throw himself toward the window. Red-faced, he bangs his hand against it and screams, "Fucking *go*, already!"

Hugh recoils from sight and stands there a minute, unsure whether to keep waiting or just leave. Cold water drips down the back of his neck and under his jacket, but he doesn't move.

You deserve this, he thinks. *You fucking drunk idiot.*

He doesn't want to keep drinking, but doesn't want to go home, either. He thinks he knows of a bar a few blocks west called Red's, though he's not sure how, or whether he's actually been there. He opens his umbrella and steps out from under the awning.

Kelly catches him by the arm and pulls them back under.

"Are you okay?"

"Yeah," he says. "Fine."

"Max says you can come in, but he'll be watching you."

"Would that be okay?"

"That's what I just said."

"I mean, would you be okay with it?"

"Why do you think I'm out here?"

She smiles.

"How much did he tell you?"

"Just that you got pretty drunk Monday."

"Guilty." He's embarrassed, but inexplicably feels safe to laugh at himself.

She lets go of his sleeve. "Come on, let's go inside."

Hugh doesn't move.

"Max," he says, tasting the bitter name for the first time. "Max was pretty mad. Maybe we should go somewhere else? Let him cool off?"

"It's so gross out."

"We'll get a cab—or we can get drenched, whatever you prefer."

She studies him a moment then says, "All right. I'll just go tell him."

She's only going a few steps but Hugh offers his umbrella. She smiles when she takes it then walks back to the bar. His wait feels long, then becomes objectively so. *She's never coming back.* After fifteen minutes he thinks he might as well go, but she still has his umbrella and the rain's not letting up. For another minute he debates getting completely soaked and it's just long enough to let her return, carrying a small purse and twirling his open umbrella over her shoulder.

"Okay," she says. "Let's get out of here."

Hugh reaches for the handle, but she pulls away giggling and cries, "Get your own!"—and then, to his surprise, she leans into him between his torso and arm

as though the arm should be around her. The top of her
head barely passes his shoulder. She hands him the
umbrella to hold above them and he tilts it away
immediately, exposing her to the rain. She shoves him
and laughs and he swings it back over her. They're
walking toward Red's though they haven't agreed on it
yet and Hugh asks himself, *How is this happening?*—how
can she just come along, not knowing where we're
going, and how is she so at ease, even playful? *She
doesn't know me at all*, he thinks, *doesn't know what a
fuck-up I am.*

She looks up and asks, "So. How old *are* you?"

"You know I'm going to lie," he says. "But
should I say older or younger?"

Her smile vanishes.

"Why would you lie?"

He knows he wouldn't.

"I won't," he says. "I'm sorry. I thought I was
flirting."

"I'm twenty-one," she says. "I'm in my third year
at Ryerson. How do you feel about that?"

"What's your major?"

"Sociology—wait, seriously? Answer my
question."

"I don't know how I feel," he says. The full-
disclosure train is leaving the station and he can't do

anything to stop it. "I'm thirty and I've been single again for a month."

"Yeah, you're a little rusty."

"We were together nine years—I don't know what I'm doing."

"Having some fun?"

"Maybe?"

"So, you just think I'm hot, or—?"

"No—"

"You don't think I'm hot?"

"I didn't mean—"

She laughs.

"Relax," she says. "*I don't think the age thing is weird.*"

The light changes at Christie Street and they cross toward a dark, run-down bar with older, shady-looking men smoking out front.

"If you're taking me here," she says, "we might need to talk."

He nods up the street, looking just beyond the McDonald's. "I was thinking Red's."

"Yeah, it's nice."

Did she hesitate before "nice"?

They walk the last few metres without speaking, and when they enter, he doesn't recognize the bar at all. Did he read about it in some Toronto blog list, or something? He reminds himself that his confusion's not important, particularly not to Kelly, who seems comfortable at the table they've chosen, one of the few not already occupied by people mostly older than Hugh. She seems just as distracted by the Toronto sports memorabilia covering the walls as he is, or as he's trying to seem in order to avoid simply staring at her. She's beautiful. The light's brighter here than at the Syc and he sees a few freckles on her nose and cheeks he didn't notice before. She orders a vodka tonic and he takes a pint from some new microbrewery.

Ask her questions about herself.

"So why sociology?"

She says, "It's interesting," without sounding interested at all. "I could go to law school after if I wanted to."

The server brings their drinks. Kelly sucks up half of hers through a straw.

"What kind of law would you do?"

"I don't know—maybe family? My parents are divorced."

"I'm sorry."

"It was a long time ago. It's better for both of them."

"Was it better for you… and your… brother? Sister? Do you have any brothers or sisters?"

She shakes her head. He doesn't know which question she's answering and doesn't get to ask—her phone rings in her purse on the table and she retrieves it.

"Yes," she says. "Fine." She seems impatient. "No!" Her expression softens. "I will… okay… yes." She hesitates a moment, as though thinking better of saying something else, then says, "Bye," and ends the call. "Max," she says. "He really looks out for us."

"I'll say," he should not have said.

"What's that supposed to mean?"

"Nothing, I just mean—"

"Some rando from the bar comes looking for me, some guy like ten years older who's been in twice and been shit-faced both times, and he's not supposed to worry?" She swipes the phone screen a couple of times. "He wants to know I'm okay. What's wrong with that?"

"Nothing."

She noisily vibrates her lips.

"I'm pretty safe, though, as far as randos go," Hugh says.

"No kidding." She can't fight off a smile. "Look where you took me."

"You said it was nice."

"If you're sixty!" She sucks up the rest of her drink and stares into the empty glass a few seconds. "I'm sorry," she says. "I thought I was joking, it just didn't come out that way." She sighs loudly, like a teenager. "I don't know why I'm here. I should go."

"It's okay," Hugh says, but it's not and there's nothing he can do to make it so. He doesn't know why he presses on. "I know we just met, but… do you want to talk about it?" He smiles a little. "I mean, it's looking like you'll never see me again—so why not, right?"

What a relief to make her laugh.

"Max and I used to see each other, and we're talking about getting back together. He can be jealous and he's got a temper and he's even older than *you*—"

"Hey!"

"—but I don't know. I think I want to try again."

"That's why he was livid earlier, right? Because you went out with me tonight?"

"He was livid *Saturday* when I gave you my number." She frowns. "I think I did it just to piss him off—"

"For fuck's sake."

"We were fighting. Don't hate me." She stirs the ice with her straw. "I think we're better now."

They look at each other in silence a moment.

"Yeah, I'm going to go," she says. "I can't drink any more anyway, I have to drive. I left my car just over there." She points across the table, back toward Bathurst, and Hugh remembers the big lot beside the McDonald's. She'd had to walk this far anyway.

"I live with my mom in Markham," she says.

"Oh."

"She freaks out if I'm late."

She stands up and extends her arm.

"It was nice meeting you, Hugh."

"Yeah, you too," he says, accepting the handshake.

"I'd say see you around the bar, but—"

"I might stay away for a while."

"Probably a good idea," she says. "Oh, I've got to pay for my—"

"I'll get it."

She waves awkwardly and says, "Okay. Bye," then leaves without looking back.

When she's gone Hugh looks over the men at the other tables, some in groups, some alone like him, all of them older, and all at once remembers the argument after he was cut off—being shoved out the front door, Christine screaming at him, her father pretending this wasn't happening and Hugh wasn't his prospective son-in-law. This was the place. He peers into his glass, still half-full, then drains it in three quick gulps. The server rushes over to propose another drink, but Hugh's already standing and dropping cash on the table.

He deserves no better than to just go home and take his medicine—someone's waiting up for him, too.

THURSDAY

THE MUSCLES IN HIS BACK COMPLAIN as he rolls over and reaches from the bed to the floor. He really needs a night table. His phone displays the time, *11:08*—ten hours, he realizes. Ten uninterrupted hours of sleep, but still he feels off. He makes his way to the bathroom, remembering how he did it: expired night-time cold medicine, blindly dumped from the lone bathroom drawer that was his in the house into a box and which, serendipitously, wound up on top of the assortment when the box was emptied in handfuls into the apartment's shallow medicine cabinet. It was the kind of pill Christine wouldn't touch even before its expiry date, and though she hated when he used it, it did the job— it and the five drinks, in last night's case. There are two pills left. He might try it again tonight.

He's slept, but he's unsatisfied, and he thinks it's the half-erection he's had since he woke. Why didn't the woman come? He thinks of her pale skin and black hair, red lips and the vague shape of her body, but other details are left to his imagination. In the night, he hasn't seen whether her nipples are pink or dark, her areolas the size of dimes or drink coasters or whether she shaves. He's never heard her voice, though by the time he enters the hot shower and grips his cock there's something like it in his head saying *give it to me, do it, do it now* and when he moans, she does, too.

She didn't actually visit, though, he reminds himself, she only appeared in his imagination—

And then he thinks, *Those probably aren't different things.*

He puts on a rather new T-shirt and rather old jeans then sends me another text.

So it didn't go well with Kelly at all. Also I lost my mind and tore up that door in the kitchen. I'm getting kicked out at the end of the month. But the ghost woman didn't come last night so at least I got some sleep. She must see how fucking pathetic I am too. Are you working in town this weekend? Do you want to do something? I swear I'll keep it together. Ugh. Sorry. Let me know.

*

When he sent the message I'd been on-set for a few hours already, mixing vats of blood for a cold-case show re-enacting an axe murder. It was grisly shit. The schedule was ambitious, and one of the actors hadn't understood what she was being cast for and took a long time to get comfortable with the scene. By lunch, when I saw Hugh's text, I already knew we'd finish late.

Jeet and another craft we've known for years, Anthony, were going to see this black metal band play, on Dundas, west of Chinatown. Anthony said we couldn't miss it, and we trusted him. The band had reunited for the first time since the nineties, when they were a huge deal, apparently. Jeet and Anthony couldn't wait, while I was pretty sure I'd never heard of them. I don't think I cared. Jeet and I started going to these shows for the spooky shit—the make-up, the blood, the noise—but we weren't too into the music or the ultra-serious crowd, standing stock still and reverent save for a few slam-dancers that everyone else seemed annoyed with. It's usually the same few, Anthony says, and some of these people are actual shithead Nazis. It's good that Jeet's huge. At a lot of shows, he and Hisayo are the only people who aren't white.

When I sent Kate a text to check in, she wrote what she'd said on Hugh's moving day: *It's not like the baby's going to come tonight.* I realize now, this time might've been sarcastic, but as I had to be back at work early the next morning anyway, I said I'd likely stay over. She answered just, *Ok.*

For a long time, staying over meant Jeet's pull-out couch, but since he moved in with Hisayo, I've stayed with them less. Some of it is that once you have a kid, even if he's asleep and you'll leave for work before he wakes up, you still just have to come home—but some of it's Hisayo, too. Jeet wouldn't have minded me crashing, but he and I used to party pretty hard, and though Hisayo stayed civil, I think she got tired of it, especially after the last time, when I was sick—in the toilet, not on the living room carpet or anything. They didn't say *Never again,* but it seemed understood. And while I suppose I could've asked Anthony, he's a bit intense for me. For example, I find it funny when Bart Simpson says, in church, "All the best bands are affiliated with Satan," but I don't think Anthony sees the humour in *Her Majesty's Satanic Request* or *We Sold Our Souls for Rock and Roll* or even *Highway to Hell.* Cartoon devil horns are enough for me. Anthony's place might be covered in pentacles.

Plus, from Hugh's text, it seemed he needed company more than Anthony did. I think Christine banned me after I caused Hugh to stand her up that one time, or maybe he just knew not to ask her again, but now he had his own place and things had gone alright Saturday. Atop the text conversation, I tapped the phone icon.

"Hey man," he said, "I'm so glad you called, shit's so fucked up, I'm losing my mind—" He caught his breath. "What's up?"

He was in for the concert. When I asked to stay, though, he said he wasn't sure it was a good idea, then buttoned up.

"The woman," he finally said.

After a few more silent seconds, I understood he didn't mean Kelly.

"She's not real," I said. "None of this stuff is. You're stressed and your mind's playing tricks on you."

"Did you see her? In front of the building on Sunday?"

"I saw a woman," I said. "But honestly, there's no way—"

"No, you're right," he said. "Of course there isn't."

He went quiet again however, and I couldn't tell if he believed me.

I hated to press, but I had nowhere else to stay.

"So, can I—"

"Yeah."

We planned for dinner at Lakeview Restaurant; I'd be late, but Hugh could meet Anthony there, who got off earlier that day and would be easy to pick out with his long, grey beard and obviously dyed, black hair, likely wearing a black T-shirt with the name of the band we were seeing in illegible white writing. Jeet and Hisayo would join later and I'd be the last, but we'd have time to eat and could walk to the show after.

I hung up, happy that Hugh was coming. He could stand to meet some new people.

*

Is it ghosts he doesn't believe in, Hugh thinks, *or is it me?* He knows it's asking a lot to drag me into his meltdown, but can't think of anyone else who won't call him crazy, from a psychiatrist or any kind of doctor to his boss or even his parents. In his adult life, he's never asked his parents for help, and he's not going to start with this.

If I can't help him, he'll have to figure it out himself.

In the *X-Files* episode, Mulder turned to some occult books in his office; on TV, there's always a handy reference, but in real life, where do you start? He opens the web browser on his phone, dreading the complete nonsense he's about to read, but he doubts this—what was the word again?—was made up for a single TV show. He types *x files sucubus* and the search engine adds the second "c" as fast as it spits results, linking to a video with six-figure likes near the top. Hugh shrugs and plays it.

The haunting music isn't the *X-Files* theme, but it's pretty close, and in a few seconds the host appears on screen and reflexively barfs, "What's up, you guys?", the only opener that seems allowed in online video before the inevitable string of follow, like and subscribe requests for all his other channels. The jump-cuts at the end of every sentence jar Hugh and he rises from the couch. He sets the phone on the kitchen counter. He'll just listen while he cleans up door debris.

"Let me say up front," the host says. "This episode *sucks*. I mean, that last scene with the assassin? It was just lazy. And the red coat thing? Total rip-off from *Don't Look Now*, this seventies movie with Donald Sutherland—"

Hugh doesn't know it.

"—based on a story by Daphne du Maurier."

He doesn't know the name.

"You know, *The Birds*? *Rebecca*?"

He's never watched any Hitchcock.

"*Don't Look Now.* Donald Sutherland and Julie Christie play a married couple whose little girl drowns—so sad!—and though they move to Venice afterward and think they can start over—yeah, right!—the man keeps seeing a girl in a red coat like his daughter had. He tries a few times to catch up to her and when he finally does, she turns out to be this hag who's trying to kill him—well, maybe not a hag, more of a dwarf, but whether it's a hag, a succubus, a nightmare, it's a trope you'll find all over the world."

Hugh looks up at just the right moment to see a definition overlay the picture.

Trope: a significant or recurrent theme; a motif

"In the Canadian province of Newfoundland, and the west of England before that,"—an image of a book cover appears in a top corner, *The Withered Arm* by Thomas Hardy, and the host points at it—"we're talking about an actual woman who leaves her body to sit on your chest while you sleep—"

Hugh snatches up the phone, presses pause and sends me a text.

Hey Newf. Remind me tonight to ask you about the hag

*

Don't misunderstand: I told you, I don't really believe in ghosts or demons or anything like them. My mother might've, though. When I was a kid, she'd tell me if I didn't shape up, a hag would get me in the night.

She moved here from Newfoundland when she was barely eighteen, met my dad and married him right away, and had bits of all kinds of stories, what I guess you'd call folklore. The hag felt the realest, and realer still when Grandma came to visit. Grandma always had one more story stranger and scarier than anything I or other kids knew. They came from lonely nights in the winter with nothing but a kerosene lamp, she said, stories her father learned in logging camps and on fishing trips with loads of time to pass and no entertainment, and they were so frightening because she knew them so well. She told them like they were true, and she must've believed, because over the back door of her house she hung a holed stone that she told me kept hags away.

I felt ridiculous, but when I saw Hugh's text I searched it on my phone and ordered him one, same-day shipping, fifty bucks by the time I was through.

*

"—while in Old Norse it's called *mara*, which gave us *nachtmahr* and *nightmare* in German and English. And in Hmong culture in Southeast Asia, it's *tsog tsuam*, who made the papers in the early eighties when a rash of otherwise healthy Cambodian immigrants to the U.S. started dying mysteriously in their sleep. It's what gave Wes Craven the idea for *Nightmare on Elm Street*, actually—"

Standing with his hands full of splinters he's picked up, Hugh freezes.

How many times did I tell him to watch that fucking movie?

"—but we're getting away from the episode. What it does—if not well!—is put a sexual dimension into the phenomenon, which not a lot of classic nightmare stories do. The *mara*, the hag, is usually old-looking, wrinkly, long-fingered and rail thin, though sometimes pudgy, too—I guess because of the weight on the chest thing. It'd be weird for a skinny girl to feel heavy."

Weird and true…

"—but the whole incubus-succubus thing, it's spurious at best. It goes back to medieval times and this, how shall I say—crackpot!—text called *Malleus Maleficarum*—Hammer of Witches—a how-to on witch-hunting that reconciles or maybe bastardizes Augustine and Aquinas' theories about how Satan could take on a body. Some studies even argue the whole concept's a weird leftover from a desperate attempt to prove angels can take on human bodies and therefore, the Holy-capital-letter-Ghost could, too, as that guy Jesus allegedly did—"

Hugh's not shocked by the irreverence, he wasn't raised with religion. *Crackpot* and *allegedly* were exactly the words his parents used around Christianity.

"—On the whole, all it accomplished was to get inconveniently pregnant women burned at the stake: the husband who got cheated on said, 'It was the devil!' and everyone got out the torches and straw. But to this day people still think they get visited: there are forums all over the internet about it, people scared this demon they're seeing in their dreams will kill them or the rival, which is to say the person's spouse or what have you.

"But again, I'm getting away from the episode—"

Hugh taps Pause again then types *succubus forum* into a browser window, and as though he hasn't just heard of them, he's surprised to see pages upon pages of hits. He clicks a few at random. Most use a font like comic sans, and many the same image: a painting of a fair-haired woman in white on her back with a squat goblin or something on her chest and a black horsehead in the background. Posts fall into categories equating to "What's happening to me?", "How do I make this stop?" and the pervier "How do I summon a succubus?" A lot of the signatures link to self-published novels.

crunchy81
ive had a succubus 4-5 yrs and now i have a girlfriend and i'm worried she'll get violent (the succubus not the gf) – like in that movie the entity, anyone see that?

bigrod
barbara hershey's boobs = awesome

DrEquity
@bigrod Yeah, rape is awesome, isn't it? You're a cretin.

bigrod
<<comment flagged>>

<3bloodymary<3

@crunchy81 you ever hear this podcast? might help

Hugh shrugs and clicks the link under <3bloodymary<3's reply, which takes him to a more serious-looking page. Two young, geeky men are pictured at the top-right of a banner that reads *Weird Things*, and centred below it is an episode list under the heading *First Person*; after *Alien Abduction* and *My Dead Grandmother Visited Me* is one called *Incubus and Succubus Demons*. He checks the clock and downloads the episode to play on his way to the restaurant. He can spend the rest of the afternoon reading internet nutjobs, the rest of his life if he wants to, but if the woman is real and he can't stop her anyway, it won't matter.

If he'd rather go running—which to his surprise, he would—then he may as well.

*

--Welcome back, or if it's your first time listening, welcome to Weird Things. I'm Jonathan Gregg.
--And I'm Lee Brown.
--And today we're continuing our special First Person series, in which we interview people who've had let's say, weird
--I'll say
--Weird experiences.

--Have you ever had the feeling, Jon, where you're awake but you can't move? Your eyes are open, you're aware of what's going on, you can see and hear, but you're just stuck there and there's something weighing you down?

--Myself, no. But I had a girlfriend in high school who did, or said she did.

--You had a girlfriend in high school?

--I did. Her name was Maggie and she moved to Punxsutawney senior year.

--Huh.

--Anyway, after school one day, she had a nap at my house.

--Just a nap? I mean, were your parents home?

--It wouldn't have mattered. [Laughs] Anyway, I was in the living room reading a book, doing homework, I guess, and all of a sudden I heard her. It sounded like she was crying. When I came into the room, she screamed. I said, "Maggie, what—? What is it?" and she said she thought I was someone else. I asked, "Who?" and she said, "I don't know. This huge guy with this really ugly face was leaning over me and I was so scared, I couldn't breathe." I got into the bed and she hugged me and said, "I couldn't move. I was staring at him, and he was leaning down closer and closer to me, and I couldn't move, I couldn't say anything."

--Weird.

--Yeah. Weird. I held onto her and tried to calm her down—said, "It's okay, it was just a dream," that kind of thing—and, I don't know, I guess it never happened again.

--Never?

--Well, she moved to Punxsutawney, so I don't know. Hey, you know, magic of the internet, anyone could be listening anywhere—Maggie, if you hear this, send us an email and let us know!

--I'm telling your wife.

--She'll hear the show before you get the chance, Jon. My wife loves the show.

--Well, our guest today said she loves the show, too. She got in touch in the spring, when we first asked listeners to tell us about weird things that had happened to them for this special series. She didn't want us to use her real name—

--We'll call her Shirley.

--Don't call me Shirley. But she said she had always been too embarrassed to tell anyone about it, and had kept this secret a long time—and her experience sounds pretty similar to Maggie's. Let's have a listen:

--"I would wake up—I know I was awake, I could see my bedroom and the posters on my ceiling—"

--"How old were you then?"

--"Seventeen, I think."

--"Go on."

--"And I would be frozen there. Then I would hear this tapping sound."

--"Like what?"

--"Like knocking on the door, almost. It would get closer, and this black figure would loom over me. He had sharp teeth and a really long nose and he smelled awful."

--"And what would happen then?"

--"The pressure on me would just get heavier and heavier until I thought I would die."

--"So were you scared?"

--"At first, yes."

--"At first?"

--"Well, I got so used to it. For a while it happened… maybe three nights a week?"

--"How long did that go on?"

--"I'd say a couple of months."

--"But it got less scary?"

--"Well, that's what was embarrassing. I came to like it after a while."

--"The feeling that you were going to die?"

--"Well, maybe not that part of it."

--"I don't understand."

--"Well, life is just so boring. I mean, I'm sixty-six now, and married—I met my husband for the first time later that year, we'll celebrate our forty-seventh wedding anniversary next year—"

--"Congratulations."

--"Thank you."

--"But you were saying…"

--"Yes. Well, it was… it was exciting. Like, [whispers] sexually. The first couple of times I was scared, but once I realized the man wasn't going to hurt me I started to enjoy it. It was kind of like the first time with my husband, actually, only, more… powerful, I guess. I would get all hot and bothered, lying there while this thing loomed over me—"

--"Not actually having sex with you, though?"

--"No. No, my first time was definitely with my husband."

--"So, doing what, then?"

--"I don't know. Teasing me, in a way? I mean, he would kind of fade and disappear and I would be left there and I'd tremble a little and put my hands on my chest and I'd be in this cold sweat and out of breath and—oh, you must think I'm nuts, huh?"

--"Not at all. Our show is called Weird Things."

--"Well it was definitely weird."

--"And you said it went on for a couple of months?"

--"Yes."

--"And how did it stop?"

--"I don't know. [pause] I remember a week or so where every night I was expecting the man to come again and was surprised when he didn't [laughs]—and maybe a little sad, too—and I remember waiting for him some mornings, with my mother calling up the stairs to my

bedroom while I would lie there and quietly saying the name I had given him, 'Philip,' over and over again."
--"Why Philip?"
--[long pause] "I don't remember."
--"And when Philip never came again?"
--"I don't know. I guess I just didn't think about it anymore. A thought of him would come into my mind once in a while, but as time went on the only thought that came with it was always, 'Wow, I hadn't thought of that in a long time' [pause]. It was so long ago. I met my husband and started planning the wedding, and then we had the wedding, and then…"

*

"Anthony?"

"You're Bobby's friend," the other replies with no change to his expression.

He was easy to identify and it wasn't just the sad dye job; in the dining room with the art deco, black-and-formerly-white floor, he was the only customer, seated in a wood booth and wearing the T-shirt I said he would be.

Hugh says his own name and offers his hand, which Anthony shakes. Neither says anything for a minute. A server with glasses and a mustache comes and asks, "Another soda water?"

Anthony says, "Sure."

"And for you?"

"I was going to get a beer…"

"Don't let me stop you," Anthony says.

Hugh orders a glass almost at random and when the server leaves, he asks, "How do you know Bobby?" just to say something. He knows we work together.

Anthony says, "Work."

"What do you do?"

Now he smiles. "Everything."

Hugh waits.

"Prosthetics. Aliens, poked-out eyes, melted faces."

"Gross," Hugh says.

"But fun."

"Horror movies?"

"More Sci-Fi lately, but enough horror."

The drinks arrive and Hugh's not sure if it's weird to say "Cheers" with a non-alcoholic drink.

Anthony cocks an eyebrow and raises his glass. "Hail Satan?"

"Pardon?"

"Cheers," he says.

"Cheers," Hugh says, bringing his glass to his mouth right away to buy time. *What do I say now?*

"So do you go to a lot of heavy metal shows?"

"Pffft. Heavy metal shows. Cavemen in circle pits." He sets down his glass and holds out both fists, showing off single letters tattooed between the lower knuckles on each finger to read *T-R-V-E* and *C-V-L-T*. "These are rituals. This is black metal."

"Like, Black… Sabbath?"

"Oh—no."

Hugh has no response, but thankfully the door jingles and Jeet's voice fills the dining room. He's in the black leather vest he always wears when goes out, over a black T-shirt that shows off the viny tattoos down both his arms. He stops talking to Hisayo—he's always talking, she doesn't say much—and introduces himself and his girlfriend.

Anthony says, "I was just telling Hugh about black metal. He's never been, he has no idea—wait, have you? I suppose I just assumed."

"No, you're right," Hugh says.

Anthony pulls his beard into a long point under his chin. "You didn't even google it?" He can't wait to explain, but Jeet says, "Probably for the best—looking into it can scare you off, with all the media focus on the satanism and church-burning—"

The what?

"—but that was really just this one group in Norway."

"And some in Sweden," Anthony says. He points at his T-shirt. "These guys are from Sweden."

"They wear the corpse paint," Hisayo says, gesturing to her face. "White and black."

Like KISS, Hugh thinks, but suspects he shouldn't say. He's wearing a green golf shirt and stands out beside these three—Hisayo, too, is all in black, a bustier under a fishnet top.

"But not like KISS," Anthony says, less confrontational than when Hugh arrived. He's fine once you get to know him. His tone changes so he sounds more like a teacher. "Black metal vocals are shrieked, or roared. Everything's lo-fi and distorted as fuck. The guitarists are shredding and a lot of the time there's an ominous synth—"

"KISS had synth on some albums," Jeet says.

"And they were justly crucified for it."

Jeet snickers. Like he does at work, he's winding Anthony up. For Hugh, he adds, "*Crazy Nights.* It's a horrible album."

Anthony says, "If this band met Gene Simmons, they'd literally crucify him."

Hugh's phone buzzes, from me: *Won't make it to eat, meet you at the show.* Work was done for the day, but I had to call Kate; this close to delivering, walking Cole to and from daycare took about all the energy she had. I didn't mind the call—it actually helped me feel less guilty about not being home—but on a night out, inevitably, it meant a half-hour of getting antsier in the driver's seat with every *Yeah* and *Uh-huh* I provided, not really listening and just wanting just to turn the key and get off the lot.

*

East of Ossington on Dundas, business signs in Portuguese give way to dog grooming, organic food, indie coffee and pop-up kitchens, and in colder weather, the hipsters cede their place in Trinity Bellwoods to people with nowhere else to go who drink the same beer in the same tall cans. There's a 7-Eleven beyond the park, and a concentration of laundromats and Vietnamese restaurants-slash-karaoke joints, and a few new, basically illegal marijuana dispensaries open indefinitely between raids, and then there's a boxy old office building with a light-up beer sign hung a whole storey above an abandoned pub.

Last in his foursome, Hugh climbs the stairs, buys a twenty-dollar ticket, then peels off for the drink line. On the stage, no one's playing, and while he waits, songs he knows are cranked, the last bit of *Enter Sandman* then *Back in Black*, which transports him years into the past, to the campus bar. The singer in the tribute band was dressed as Bon for the first half, then Brian Johnson for the second, and beyond the entrance in the new flat cap, Hugh doesn't remember much—the rest of the closest thing to a metal show he's ever attended is a drunken smear, like so many other nights since he left home.

He can make it up to himself, though. See the genuine article. He wouldn't go without Christine, before—and she'd never have come with him—but now he doesn't have to justify it, doesn't have to hear again that the music he likes is for dinosaurs as though, years ago, she didn't scream along as loudly as he did to *Hell's Bells*. (That part he'll never forget.) *And Bobby could go with me*, he thinks—he doesn't have to defend me to her anymore, either. He doesn't know tonight that he missed AC/DC in Toronto the fall before, or that the real band is already a tribute band—the drummer's been arrested and fired, one of the Young brothers has been replaced on guitar by his nephew after a massive stroke, and on the last leg of the tour Axl Rose is filling in now that Brian's nearly deaf and suddenly retired—but if Hugh asked, I'd still go with him. Who do you think bought him that *Highway to Hell* cassette for his fifteenth birthday?

When his turn comes, he orders two Fifties in tall cans, but the line behind Hugh isn't long and he scolds himself. One at a time should be enough. He spots his new friends and sees their group has grown by one.

She has pale skin, and long, black hair.

Bright red lips.

His grip dents both the cold, sweaty cans. *How will she do it this time? Knock me out in the bathroom, or wait till I'm droopy-eyed drunk then pounce from the mosh pit…?*

"HUGH!!"

He isn't paralyzed this time, he's just been standing and staring in the direction of his new friends for… he doesn't know how long.

He looks over his shoulder to where he heard his name then mutters, "Shit."

Peter emerges from the still-sparse crowd and stands in front of him, double-fisting tall cans of his own. He's wearing the Swedish soccer team's yellow jersey.

"I know, I should be resting at home…"

"No way! No one should miss this band!" Peter cups his hand around his mouth and yells, "*SVER-YA!*" How'd he even have *time* to get this drunk between work and now?

"I wouldn't sleep anyway," Hugh says softly.

"Right! Your mara."

"What did you say?"

"*Mara*—the woman, that's what we call her in Sweden."

Has Peter believed him all along?

"I wasn't going to say anything. I think it's a stupid old wives' tale and won't help you. But after we talked, I remembered my grandmother telling me about it." He looks around. "So are you out rebounding? Because there are places with more women—like, literally any other place."

Hugh glances up at his dinner companions and the dark-haired woman still standing with them.

Peter follows his eyes.

"The Japanese girl?"

"No, that's Jeet's girlfriend—friends of a friend, I came with them. I should get back there."

"Then the other one? Don't tell me she's with the super-old guy..."

"You see her, too!" Hugh blurts out.

Peter, unphased, just replies, "Fuckin' fox." He shines with sweat and stands awkwardly as though his balance is off. "Let's go meet her."

Hugh's not sober, either, but feels a small charge maybe not caused by alcohol. His shoulders relax and his cheeks warm. "I think I'll go alone," he says. The courage dissipates as he approaches, though. He's carrying beers three and four of the night at—what is it, eight-thirty?—and none of my friends have even been to the bar yet. He edges in beside their circle.

The woman is first to make eye contact.

"You must be Hugh." She smiles. "Is one of those for me?"

Her teeth aren't so pointy.

Hugh says, "Sure," smiling awkwardly and offering her his left can because he hasn't drunk from it yet.

She leans in and takes his right. "I only just met you."

Do I come across that way? Like I would drug a drink? Or is that just what women have to do?

"I'm Becca," she says.

Jeet and Anthony are shouting a conversation from which Hugh can only pull small parts, mostly morbid phrases he can only assume are band names. He needs to look somewhere other than Becca and the orange-outlined *KISS* across the chest of her black T-shirt. Has she taken grief from Jeet and Anthony about it yet? So far, she seems to listen more than talk—or maybe she doesn't listen at all. He wants to touch her and not just in the way you think. He wants to be sure this isn't the prelude to another knockout and pair of jizz-stained shorts.

She puts a hand on his shoulder, gently, but still he flinches.

"Which band are you most excited to see?"

He tries to recall even one name from the bill he didn't look at, then finally spews, too enthusiastically, "All of them!"—and *then*, as though it explains something, adds, "I've never seen any of them before!"

Does she see me wincing? It's already a dark room and mercifully, it gets darker. Some scattered cheers bounce off the walls as four lanky men with long, dark hair stalk from the wings to a guitar, bass, synth and drumkit onstage. They don't say a word, don't count off or anything, just come in all together on a barrelling double-kick and a guitar so distorted that the fast strumming makes a sound more like a drone than a note. Synth and bass further oppress in the bottom end. An emaciated-looking fifth man enters the scene, the lead singer with hair longer and straighter than the others. His face is made-up in white with dark circles around the eyes and black lines down his cheeks like cracks in a windshield. He grips the microphone and shrieks and Hugh's not sure whether the words are in English. Near the stage, some dudes form a circle and start slamming into each other.

"It's actually my first time," Hugh confesses loudly. "I don't know what to do."

Becca gestures toward the pit. "Those guys will show you around."

"I think I'll steer clear." He smiles, strangely unafraid to admit he's afraid.

Becca returns the smile and says, "Me, too." She looks behind them and Hugh follows her gaze: two chairs at the back of the room. "Do you want to—"

"Yes!" He's too eager again, but she doesn't seem to mind. They weave through the crowd with her one hand trailing just enough to make Hugh think he should hold it.

"So what do you do, Hugh?" she asks after they sit down beside each other. She can't finish the question without laughing. "Ugh! I hate that one."

"Because you don't like what you do?"

"No," she says. "I'm an ER resident at St. Mike's. I love what I do—I mean, I never sleep, but I love it." She leans closer to his ear. "But I asked you first."

"I lay out grocery store flyers."

"So, you're a graphic designer?"

"Officially," he says. "But it's kind of the same thing every week."

"I have a friend who does websites," she says. "He never goes to an office." She lightly grips his forearm. "You don't have to go to the office tomorrow, do you?"

For once, he doesn't. He swirls the last of the beer in his can then drains it.

"Which band did you come to see?" he asks.

She grins and gushes, "All of them!"

Hugh laughs. "Yeah, busted. I'm not into this at all."

"Me neither."

"What are you doing here, then?"

"I like fish out of water."

"Do I stand out that much?"

"Oh, yeah." She sets her beer down on the table. "It's nice when it goes fast, though. The last thing I want is to still be here at two o'clock, trying to decide which drunken loser to leave with." She gestures toward where Peter was standing, where a fist pumps in the air above a yellow blur that's colliding with everyone. "It was already down to you or him." Hugh's a bit offended—he doesn't feel like a loser tonight, at least not yet—but she's pulling him in. If it doesn't matter to her that he's drunk, then maybe it shouldn't to him either.

"Do you want to… go?" he asks.

"Please."

He surveys the room and sees the trio he'd come with head-banging, even seemingly reserved Hisayo. He doesn't see me, though, or remember that I'm supposed to be staying with him. He doesn't think of me at all—he just follows Becca as though she has a leash on him, down the stairs into the cold air where a cab pulls up.

Becca gets in first, sliding across the bench as the driver asks, "Where are you going?"

"Where do you live?" she asks Hugh.

"My place is… uh…"

"Oh no—you're married, aren't you?"

"No! No, it's… I just moved in and there's crap all over—"

"Divorcing?"

"Dumped," he says, surprised at his frankness.

Becca sighs and says, "Three hundred Brunswick." The car starts moving.

"Sorry," Hugh says. "I—"

She puts a hand over his mouth and says sweetly, "I don't actually care."

They turn north onto Bathurst and follow a streetcar, unable to get past it before the right onto Bloor. In the Annex, every second front's a bar; Thursday night's in full swing and packs of university-aged people roam the sidewalks smoking and wearing too little clothing to keep warm. The cab stops in front of an infamous, dumpy bar that's dark and empty, mercifully closed since the spring. Tens of thousands of drunken hook-ups have begun at this intersection, but somehow Hugh's first in Toronto has ended up here. Becca pays the driver then shimmies across the seat, holding Hugh's right arm with two hands to get out then steering him south. "It's just there," she says, grinning and not even trying to hide her teeth.

FRIDAY

THE BEDROOM WALLS ARE DEEP PINK and slightly sunlit in the same colour. The ceiling's free of cracks. He's on his back, his brow slick with sweat, the rest of his body clammy. *Not now*, he thinks, realizing where he is. *Please, not now.* He summons the strength to move a hand over his crotch—a hand that doesn't resist, and finds the rim of the condom he's still wearing.

The door opens and Becca's eyes fall on the tented comforter. She says, "Well, I was going to make breakfast…" then removes her old T-shirt, the only thing she's wearing. She climbs onto the bed and leans over him, runs fingertips down his right arm then removes the condom. He should reach for another in the nightstand but as she descends on him, he's powerless to try. She puts her hands on his chest and takes him slowly but easily inside. With a small moan, he lets out the breath he's been holding. He thinks he's all the way in but she keeps descending, swallowing him up until he can't feel any other part of his body. She's not *bouncing* or *riding* or anything women in porn do on top; if he could, he'd sit up and wrap his arms around her, but her hands on his shoulders keep him immobile on his back. He's an object with a single purpose now, and it's not one of his own. A vibration grows in his chest and his throat feels like it's closing, then she pulls him up and buries his face in long, black hair at the side of her neck. It chokes his cry as he comes and she comes with him.

Arms still around her, he exhales from the bottom of his lungs and a guttural noise escapes. She backs her head up to look at him and her eyes laugh, so his mouth does, too. They untangle themselves and he reclines to lay his head on the pillow.

Becca lies on her side and rests her head on his chest. It's a different weight than has held Hugh down lately, but he can't get up now, either—not even if he wanted to.

*

"I just—" he says later, sitting on the bed in just boxers and socks. "I just feel like I have to tell you this." He partly hopes she hasn't heard him while another part of him prays she has.

Becca laughs. She's been to the shower and put on scrubs for her shift. "I've heard them all, you know. If you don't want to do this again you don't have to."

"I think I'd like to see you again."

"You think? What, you're not sure?"

"Would you like to?"

"It depends," she says. Her eyes dart to his left hand. "If you're married and your ring's just in your jeans—"

"No. But… the mess wasn't why we couldn't go to my place." He feels his face tighten. "You should know, before this goes any further—"

"Who said anything about that? I was just having fun."

His face hasn't relaxed yet.

She smiles and says, "Go on," then mock-sternly adds, "No promises."

"I've been seeing… someone…" he says.

"You still have a girlfriend." She bends down to pick his shirt off the floor. "Bye, Hugh."

"I don't," he says. "I swear. What I mean is… This is going to sound weird but please, hear me out."

She proffers the polo. "Get dressed while you tell me, in case I don't like it."

Hugh launches in about Christine as he stands and pulls the shirt over his head, saying probably too much about Christine and catching himself going on about what a douche Chase is before starting to describe the new apartment, the force pinning him to his bed, the bouncing breasts in the wet dreams he's humiliated to hear himself recounting, the brownouts, the nails, what a succubus is and the fact that in just a couple of weeks, he'll need to find a *new* new apartment.

He buckles his belt. "I'm sorry," he says. "You must think I'm nuts." He moves to the door and reaches for the knob.

"Idiopathic sleep paralysis," Becca says.

He doesn't understand, but he turns back.

"It means its cause is unknown—well, it's clear what causes the paralysis, basically your brain wakes up before your body does—but it happens to lots of people, and they don't usually know why." She smiles again. "My hypothesis is, you really needed to get laid."

Hugh raises his eyebrows.

"I *am* a doctor," she says.

He still can't imagine trying to explain this in a doctor's office.

"So what can I do?"

"Get some sleep, ironically." She twitches her nostrils and Hugh can tell it's her tic when she diagnoses. "It probably won't last, and it's likely to do with stress. Take some time off work, sleep in, maybe don't drink for a few days, eat some vegetables, get a massage… There's no guarantee it'll help, but it can't hurt."

"So, second date, vegetarian and massages?"

"First date. You don't get to count last night." She glances at the alarm clock on the nightstand and says, "I've got to go." Hugh starts to ask when he can see her again, but stops when she grabs his hips and takes his phone from a side pocket. She types a little as she walks to the front door with Hugh following then gives the phone back. "You just asked me out," she says. "I'll reply eventually. Three-day rule and all that."

She pulls him into her by his collar and whispers, "If I can wait that long."

*

It doesn't matter that they left the concert early—his ears are ringing. The massive coffee he bought on the way home is cold but still half-full. He moves his computer off his lap and rises from the couch, taking the paper cup to the kitchen, where he dumps it into a mug he puts in the microwave. When he removes it and closes the door, the clock reappears. It's not even ten, but it feels like four in the afternoon, when on workdays his focus usually drifts away from flyer-making. He's already wandered around the internet this morning, though, and deliberately avoided autocompletes leading back to the succubus forums, the weirdos he found himself believing just a day ago. He longs for more boxes to unpack, more tedium to occupy his mind, then sees the cardboard still piled by the door and realizes he needs tape, now, to put them back together. In three weeks, he'll be moving again.

He looks a second longer. *Is that…?*

A corner of the T-shirt from Monday is sticking out from under the waste.

How often has he been in and out since then, and how'd he drop the cardboard on it without even seeing it? That must be where he took it off Monday, if in fact *he* took it off—

And then he decides. It doesn't matter that he can't remember walking home or removing the shirt or leaving it there. He did these things just like he did what Christine said he did, even if he can't remember, even if he won't let himself—and if he could call them aberrations, brief lapses in self-awareness, it still wouldn't mean he hadn't been a shit. She said he had, so he had, and his rationalizing made about as much sense as a sex demon being responsible for a misplaced T-shirt.

Idiopathic, Becca said, *cause unknown*—a valid medical explanation, somehow.

The dirty shirt gets picked up and tossed into the pile a laundry hamper will replace when he buys one, and from the dresser he pulls another beer case freebie and pair of shorts.

Today he'll run so far nothing chasing him will ever catch up.

*

Two kilometres—a mere two kilometres and he's gassed, chest heaving, the back of his thigh cramping. He leaves the path and crosses the park through the big grass bowl in the centre, where on summer evenings young people play ultimate frisbee and weekend mornings a cricket game is often found, not that Hugh's seen either yet. He removes the buds from his ears and in the fenced section behind him, dogs yip as they play. The park's quiet otherwise. He climbs the hill to Heathdale Road, where big, old, brick houses get stripped and then built into bigger-looking black cubes, their sloped roofs now flat and their driveways accessorized with a Porsche and a Land Rover. This will never be his life. In his building of the same age, just around the corner, nails won't even stay in the floorboards. Do these people just work harder than him? He thinks of his own job for the first time today. Only the weekend stands between him and a first-thing meeting to tell Peter everything's okay now, by which he'll mean he just won't mention this haunting business again.

Not "*haunting,*" he reminds himself: not a ghost, not a dead person, just a thing that rides him in the night.

A hag, he recalls, then stops walking and says, "Oh fuck…"

He takes his phone from his pocket—"*fuck-fuck-fuck-fuck-fuck…*"—then finds the texts I sent the night before.

He presses Call but it doesn't ring, it just clicks straight through to voicemail.

*

Hugh tries this evening but can't remember the last day he didn't drink. Does that make him an alcoholic? He doesn't have the shakes—he's *never* had the shakes—but he's restless. He looks at the whiskey, still on the counter from Wednesday, but can't make himself pour it.

That's good, he thinks.

But the boredom. How long has it been since he's gone out on a Friday night? Isn't that what he's supposed to be doing now, going out and picking up women or something? He doesn't know. He didn't pick up Christine—if anything, she went after him—and now it seems Becca has, too. But why? He's not what you'd call irresistible, and he knows it; in fact, aging, boring, possible alcoholic Hugh Campbell seems pretty easy to stay away from. So, what? At a violent metal show, did he just seem like the safe one?

And if he gets angry again—will he be safe then?

Like I said at the beginning, I haven't talked to him in a long time. I don't know how it turns out, but I tell myself this is the moment: he looks at the bottle again, but goes for a walk instead.

At St. Clair he turns right, but not before looking the other way a moment. What's behind the Syc's lit-up window that he wants? It's not Kelly, it's not Max pounding his face in, and thinking about it while he walks west, no, he doesn't just want to drink, either. Past a paint shop, then the McDonald's, he comes to Red's, where through the windows, he sees a small crowd around the tables, standing room only, for the band pressed against the wall and bleeding *Free Fallin'* into the street. They've got enough sad old dudes in there tonight.

After Red's, he has no destination in mind and no idea how long he might walk. Businesses begin to alternate between newer, upscale shops and dark fronts with sheets in the windows, where they have windows—some upper floors have solid façades and he thinks they must have been theatres before, which I can confirm, they were. A cinema would be perfect for Hugh tonight, if only because it likely wouldn't have a liquor licence, but all that's here is side street after side street that leads to old, working-class houses. Both sides of St. Clair are dead zones of fenced-off lots and low, boxy showrooms for condos that probably won't be built.

And then, just in front of him, is a run-down video store.

He asks himself, *What are the chances…?*

From the cluttered entrance he spots the *HORROR* sign, under which—he's in luck—is a battered *Nightmare on Elm Street* DVD. He brings it to the counter to pay and it takes just seconds to open an account: name, driver's licence, phone number, the way it was the last time he rented a movie, however many decades ago that was.

Not ready to confront the whiskey bottle and whatever—whoever—waits at home, he keeps walking until the assortment of shops changes to old-fashioned clothing stores, pizzerias and cafés, all with Italian names. From Dufferin, he'll take the streetcar back. He waits at the island stop while a distant, green light becomes the two above the windshield of the approaching streetcar. It squeals to a stop and its doors hiss open. He sits at the back and takes his phone from his pocket, unsure what he's looking for, just hoping to pass the time.

He has a text from Becca, received half an hour ago.

I want to come over. Your place can't be that bad

He replies, *I just rented a movie if you want to watch it with me*

The phone vibrates.

Who still rents movies?

A second message follows, asking for his address. He sends it and, as the streetcar lurches forward after another stop, he smiles for a second—but just a second.

What will I do if the other woman shows up?

*

He crouches and sweeps into the pan a third time then stands and eyes the fractured door jamb, the gouge in the trim. *I can't get this angry ever again*, he thinks. *It will be different with Becca.*

Or I hope that's what he thought.

At the trashcan, he feels grit under his sock—more splinters, and endless dust. Isn't cleaning the first thing you're supposed to do when you move in? He crouches again and feels his chest tightening. *I'll never finish before she gets here.* The pizza box from two nights ago gets stashed under the sink while his few dishes drip on the rack. The counter shines a little from being quickly wiped, but not properly cleaned. He's sweeping the bedroom when his phone buzzes in his pocket.

Are you home? I'm out front, the text says. He hasn't told her he has no buzzer—it's old and doesn't work with cell phones.

(He didn't tell me, either. It wouldn't have mattered if I'd buzzed the right number.)

He rushes into the hall and down the stairs, anxious he's made her wait too long. Through the glass door she smiles faintly, one hand raised in an immobile wave. He turns the handle to let her in.

"I'm sorry," he says. "The buzzer—"

"You still rent movies, but you don't have a landline? You're a mystery."

She gives him a short kiss on the mouth before he can laugh, so short she doesn't need to breathe in again to say, "Hi."

He says it back.

She points to a small brown box on the floor.

"That has your name on it."

"I didn't order anything." He lifts it, surprised at its heft. "What's in here, a rock?"

Becca smiles and he leads her to the second floor, where she pauses on the landing and looks at the pair of windows, arched at the top like the stained-glass in the few churches Hugh's entered for weddings, funerals and one time, Easter with his great-grandmother. "Gothic," she says. "Neat."

He responds, "Yeah," but the term means nothing to him.

Becca tarries again in the hall to say, "The sconces are great, too. The light's so warm."

"And dim enough to hide the dirt in the old dump."

"This isn't a dump," she says. "It's a great building. I love it."

He turns the key and the door knocks the broom he left near it to the floor. He picks it up as nonchalantly as possible and squeezes past the cardboard still stacked in the entrance.

"Oooh, did you clean up for me?"

He glances toward the kitchen then looks away again quickly, hoping she didn't follow his eyes to the knobless door that won't stay closed and now exposes the back of Number Eight's drywall, framed by splintered trim.

She did, of course, and asks, "What happened?"

I had a bad day, he almost says—as though it might absolve him, or getting angry and smashing things were okay—but instead he answers, "I thought she was coming in through there—"

"The ghost woman, or whatever?"

He nods. He can't believe he's told her, just like that—like it were completely normal. "I'm getting evicted for it," he adds, and feels strangely better when he recalls he's being punished.

"Can't you just pay for the damage?"

"I don't know." He hasn't considered it. "You must think I'm insane," he mumbles.

"It's kind of sane," she says. "I mean, where else might she come from?"

"You're too nice to me."

"Yeah, jeez. I must like you or something."

"I guess I'm not used to it."

"You and your last girlfriend were together how long?"

"Nine years."

"You must have been *okay*," Becca says.

"She was so sick of me, though. Every little thing I did—" He feels his face tensing, a flush of resentment. "I'm sorry, I shouldn't talk about it."

She pats his shoulder. "It's good to—but, maybe not to me."

"You mean a therapist, right?"

"Even just a couple of visits. You never know, you might process some other things—like, did you have any dreams as a kid? What did you want to be when you grew up?"

He thinks a minute, but honestly doesn't know.

"I think I just saw myself in an office sitting at a computer. And having a nice house, and a car, and a wife—god, I'm so boring! What could you possibly like about me?"

"You're vulnerable," she says. "A lot of guys keep their messy parts hidden until they come out in some terrible way years later. You seem comfortable with who you are."

"I'm not at all," Hugh says. "But I think I want to be."

She takes his hand and leads him to the couch, where they sit down. She rests her head on his chest for a moment.

"So, do you want to watch the movie?" Hugh asks.

"An honest talk is way better than watching a movie." She undoes the buttons of his polo shirt, grey today, and puts one hand inside on his collarbone. She eases in her second as she climbs on top of his lap.

"I don't know what to say, now."

"Not *right* now," she says, then caresses his shoulders. She kisses his neck and pulls him close.

*

Afterward, Becca has rolled onto her side and rested her head on him, and he's wrapped an arm around her. They lay like this a long time, or what feels like a long time, but it's only about twenty minutes before Becca is up and dressing again, saying she has to be at the hospital early the next day. He's invited her to stay but hasn't insisted, not afraid to seem needy but also not wanting to push his luck with this vulnerability thing. She lets him follow her to the apartment door after she's called a cab and there she whispers into a kiss, "See you soon."

The door shuts, the sound of her footsteps fades down the hall, and now Hugh's alone in his living room in just his boxers, softly illuminated by the bedroom light and no longer conscious of the curtainless windows and the minuscule chance someone might look in. There are maybe three feet between the buildings. What would someone be doing there, anyway?

He's confident, and feels himself grinning—things went well, and he doesn't just mean the sex—but then his expression droops. As much as he wanted her to stay, he forgot he couldn't have let her. *She could've been killed.* The woman could have climbed on her like she climbed on Hugh, but with no desire to please, just wanting to smother Becca and leave her dead in the bed, a message to Hugh that she is not to be trifled with—that no one else will have him.

He goes to the bathroom and runs the water, washing his face and hands in cool water. He's chosen to stop believing this nonsense but regardless, he won't sleep now. He returns to the living room where the *Nightmare* DVD is on the coffee table.

"If you're still serious," he says to probably no one, "you'll at least put the movie on for me."

He watches the plastic case, waiting for it to open, for the player's drawer to pop out and the disc to frisbee into it, the weight to pin him to his seat as the machine whirs to Play and his breath to catch in his throat, his eyes to stretch wide open to remind him he's her prisoner and she'll haunt his dreams forever. He watches another moment, though, and when he accepts the disc won't move, he attempts to get up.

With no resistance at all, he rises, opens the case, and walks it to the player.

SATURDAY

GLARING DAYLIGHT THROUGH THE WINDOW forces open his eyes. His head rests on the couch arm and his neck hurts enough to tell him he slept in this position. He sits up. The TV screen is black, save for the grey square bouncing around and telling him to *SELECT INPUT*; the DVD player shut off after the movie ended… however it ended. Hugh thinks he remembers a girl burning herself on a pipe in a dream she was having, but nothing past that—nothing about the Balinese way of dreaming or stripping a dream monster's power by just turning away from it. He reaches for the remote control, presses Off, then stands to retrieve his crumpled jeans from the floor while trying to recall where he threw his shirt—where Becca threw his shirt, maybe? He doesn't remember. He closes his eyes and breathes in through his nose deeply, thinking hard. He barely remembers the feel of her lips kissing his, her breasts in his hands or her ass atop his thighs—it was no attack, he isn't injured, he didn't drink beforehand, but still he has the sense he blacked out.

What if I'm dreaming now? he wonders. He stands and walks to the kitchen where he sees the back of the neighbour's drywall through the half-open door with the mangled latch. *Nope, this is real.*

The microwave clock shows nine-thirty: a bit early to call on a Saturday, but he has to be done with it. He finds his phone still in his pants, and Nick's name in his contacts. He taps the green icon.

"Hello?"

"Hi, Nick, it's Hugh Campbell."

Nick doesn't respond.

"I smashed up the door in my kitchen?"

"Ghost guy, right. What's up?"

"I'd like to stay," Hugh says. "And I'll pay for the damage. You won't have a problem with me again."

"It'll be expensive—"

"Or I can fix it myself."

What am I saying?

Nick says after a pause, "I've seen your work—"

"My friend's a contractor, he can help me do it."

Okay, I'm pretty good with my hands, but *contractor* was a stretch—as was the possibility we'd ever see each other again, though I didn't know it then.

Nick, eventually, says, "Fine. It's easier than getting a new tenant." Hugh hears him smile as he adds, "Especially with the ghost and all."

"I deserved that."

"When will you have it done?"

"I don't know."

"End of the month, I'll come see?"

"Sure."

"And that whole unit's due for fresh paint."

"I can do that," Hugh says.

He makes toast after hanging up, butters it and walks to the living room, where he finally spots yesterday's shirt on the floor in front of the couch, not hidden at all, beside the small package Becca found. He forgot about the box last night—he was a little distracted.

Squishing in one side, he makes space to peel the tape off the top flaps, and under the packing paper inside, sealed in transparent plastic with its label facing down is… yeah, a rock. He flips it over and reads the front, on which the largest word is *Hagstone*. At the bottom it says, *Wards off hags, witches and other evil spirits.*

He knows who it's from and tries to call again, but doesn't leave a message, assuming I'm still mad at him for leaving me to sleep in my truck the night before last. I wasn't, though. My phone just died overnight (as I tried to explain to Kate later, to no avail).

A tiny booklet tells Hugh, after a lot of pseudo-historical baloney, to hang the stone where evil is to be warded off. I mean, it's probably baloney, but whatever works, right? He stands to find his hammer, takes a mostly straight nail from the door jamb now separated from the kitchen wall, and walks to the bedroom. He centers the stone over his headboard.

*

Here he is again, sitting on the couch past midnight, desperate to close his eyes but unable to sleep. The symptom hasn't changed, but the cause is new. Becca. She texted saying she'd come after work, then again at 11:30 to say she was finally leaving. He knows it's a better kind of waiting, but it doesn't feel better yet. It won't feel better until she arrives.

He bought groceries this afternoon, after a run and a nap with no consideration of what might be on the other side of consciousness, and made a decent dinner of roasted chicken and potatoes. The leftovers are divided between two plates for lunch and dinner for tomorrow or—if he can admit he cooked *for* Becca—just lunch, as she won't have taken a break all day today and will be starving when she arrives, which he assumes is how things go when you work in emerg.

Coming home to dinner is nice, he thinks. He's missed taking care of someone, even if he's never been great at it. If this is for real, he'll have to get used to her coming in at all hours of the day and night and needing sleep or food or comfort or sex on the most idiosyncratic of schedules, but he thinks he can handle it. He can be the predictable one. This isn't at all playing it cool like Peter advised, though. And the morning after the concert, what did she say? *I was just having fun*—joking, she told him, but aren't all jokes a little true? Is he thinking too far ahead?

Maybe not. She *is* on her way over again…

He jumps when his phone buzzes—he's mostly nodded off, again losing track of *Nightmare*. If the movie didn't appeal to him as a kid, he thinks, maybe it never will. He presses pause then rushes out the door. Becca's in teal scrubs under a black jacket and carries a big, brown shoulder bag. She might have begun the day in make-up, but Hugh can't tell. He doesn't really care. He opens the door, pulsing with anticipation, and she droops into him. He holds her shoulders a moment. She looks up and says, "Hi."

Hugh kisses the top of her head before stepping out of the opening and letting the door close behind her. In the hall, they don't say anything, they just push their way into his apartment then their tongues into each other's mouths, grabbing at asses and clothing and getting half-naked on the way to the bed where they both collapse on their backs and don't move. Becca leans over Hugh and kisses his lips. He can tell she's forcing herself.

"Maybe we won't?" he says.

She rolls off him and lies on her back again.

"God, yes." She exhales. "I'm so tired."

She is human.

Hugh turns onto his side and puts an arm under her neck.

"This is really good," she says. "But I can't sleep in scrubs." She leaves the bed and takes her bag to the bathroom, returning a moment later in a silky, pale-blue nightgown. She stops in the doorway and looks above the bed.

"You actually hung something on a wall." She studies the holed stone for a moment. "But what is it?"

Hugh sighs a little. "It's stupid, I don't believe in it all"—*Am I lying?*—"but it's supposed to keep away nightmares."

Becca sits on the bed.

"And what if it scares me off?" she asks. A surprisingly sad look comes over her face.

He can't show how seriously he's taking her, how he's again thinking of how much she looks like the woman…

Oh God…

She laughs, then, snapping him out of it.

"I'm kidding! But, I kind of am a nightmare," she says. "Things start out great with guys I meet, and then my job takes over. It's still going to be tough for a couple of years." She looks at the floor. "You seem great, but this probably won't work out."

Is this what he's going to do now—pick up, hook up, break up, over and over again?

"I don't think I know how to be on my own." He didn't expect to say that, and changes focus to her. "What happens for you after you leave?"

"I go it alone for a while, till I get lonely again."

He puts an arm over her shoulder and she holds it to her chest with both hands.

"What we should be asking," she says, finally looking up at him, "is what happens if I stay."

They hold each other's gaze a moment longer, a stalemate not broken until Becca pulls away. She lies back and slides her legs under the blanket, shivering a little.

"Is the window open or something?"

Hugh knows it's not, but goes to look; it's shut, but he pushes it down anyway. He checks the lock, looks at the stone, then gets back into bed.

From behind, he wraps Becca in his arms and pulls in close to her back.

He's waiting for the chill to leave him, too.

THE DAYS AFTER

IF I'M JUST MAKING THIS UP, I can decide Hugh was fine. I can say he sobered up, because that's what I did—I'd want that for anyone, and I can't stand to think of the alternative.

He fixed the door, and Becca let her lease go and moved in, then they chose a new place that was truly for both of them. He trained for a half-marathon and ran it well enough that a marathon seemed like the next step, so he trained harder, then ran that, too. He got a better job, then a better one after that. He and Becca bought a house, and got married or had kids or both. He wrote *The Power of Tedium* and people bought it—lots of people—then he worked less and spent more time with his family. They stayed a healthy couple until one of them died of natural causes at a ripe old age—

Look, I want to give him a happy ending, to find a way to say he was all right, but with all the crap I've taken in over the years, a horror story seems to be the only kind I can tell—and settling into domesticity isn't how they end. Look at *Stepford Wives* or *Rosemary's Baby* or *Get Out* or most of Hitchcock: if anything, getting into a couple is how they start, then slowly some sinister thing creeps into the foreground and drives the protagonist mad. The explanation is always rational— that's the scariest part—but if you're telling it right, the damage can't be undone, and the audience can't be allowed to believe the evil's gone.

The last time I saw Hugh, he had a long way to go. Intimate relationships can't survive substance abuse. The addict will stay in delusion and self-absorption until they manage to escape their addiction, and with Becca, he would just repeat the same pattern as with Christine. He was doomed to codependence and heartbreak—I don't doubt it for a second. But that, like most everything else I've told you, is speculation.

In truth, I don't know what happened to him, and if I want to stay married, I'd best not find out. I worried, though, after I cut him out of my life. I wanted to get him help, but I couldn't; if making amends will cause further injury to someone (e.g., Kate), you don't do it. It took time to let that go, but once I did, I moved pretty quickly to the twelfth step, carrying the message, which I do once a week in little rooms, piecing together stories about horrors I've survived. There, too, I talk a lot about Hugh. It wasn't until he was gone for good that I realized how much I'd missed him.

I don't believe in the supernatural. I told you that up front. But I also said that every part of the story I'm physically in is true, and that includes the morning after I moved him in. I saw the dark-haired woman standing outside his building. I saw her at the show, too. No one can tell me I didn't.

And so, the way I tell a story, there's only one ending that makes sense.

We have to conclude that she got him.

ACKNOWLEDGEMENTS

This book would not exist without:

The steadfast love and support of my wife, Pauline, and the joy of our daughters, Nina and Mathilde.

The respect for creators, belief in the novella form, and genuine excitement of Chris Krawczyk and Little Ghosts Books.

The encouragement, advice, and networking prowess of Megan Beadle.

The support and friendship of the F&G Writers' Group—Julie McArthur, Nadia Ragbar, Susan Alexander, Brad Weber and Robert Shaw—on whom the myriad, messy first iterations of this story were foisted.

The time and advice of my erstwhile teacher and longtime friend, Richard Scarsbrook, and the Writers' Union of Canada's Mentorship Microgrant program that compensated him for this kind work.

The encouraging "no thank-yous" of Ron Eckel, Michael Mirolla, and Fairlight Books.

The perpetual willingness of my sibling, Dawna, to chat about ghosts and other "weird things."

The authors and academics who've dared to treat paranormal phenomena, folklore and genre fiction seriously, and thus helped me get on this field and play.

***

The alt-country song about drinking (are any of them about anything else?) is *Still Be Around*, by Uncle Tupelo. In addition to the AC/DC songs named in the text, *Shot Down in Flames* is also paraphrased. The X-Files episode referenced at length is titled *Avatar.*

The address 300 Brunswick Avenue isn't my invention, but Katherine Govier's, from her short-story collection *Fables of Brunswick Avenue*—a conceit that's proven very clever as, nearly 40 years later, there is still no such address in Toronto. I'd have never come up with this myself, but from the time I paused at Bloor and Brunswick, shortly after reading *Fables*, and confirmed the gap in the addresses, 300 Brunswick has been part of the city I live in.

The origins of Newfoundland folktales, as presented by Bobby's grandmother, are adapted from *Folktales of Newfoundland: The Resilience of Oral Tradition*, by Herbert Halpert et al. The theological origins of succubus (and incubus) demons, presented in the online video, borrows from the *Stuff to Blow Your Mind* podcast episode called *Incu-succubi: Demon in the Halls of Sleep*. The painting referred to in that scene is of course Henry Fuseli's *The Nightmare*.

The dedication comes from *Le Horla*, by Guy de Maupassant. It translates approximately to, "I was finally able to see myself, the way I do when I look at myself [in the mirror] every day". The cover image is based on several woodcuts and one painting by Edvard Munch, all of them titled *The Kiss*.

ABOUT THE AUTHOR

Daniel Perry is the author of the short story collections *Nobody Looks That Young Here* and *Hamburger,* and he lives in Toronto.

Modern Folklore is his first novel(la).